Mills & Boon
Best Seller Romance

A chance to read and collect some of the best-loved novels from Mills & Boon – the world's largest publisher of romantic fiction.

Every month, four titles by favourite Mills & Boon authors will be re-published in the *Best Seller Romance* series.

A list of other titles in the *Best Seller Romance* series can be found at the end of this book.

Violet Winspear

TENDER IS THE TYRANT

MILLS & BOON LIMITED
LONDON · TORONTO

First published 1967
Australian copyright 1968
Philippine copyright 1981
This edition 1981

© Violet Winspear 1967

ISBN 0 263 73656 3

Set in Linotype Baskerville 10 on 12 pt.

*Made and printed in Great Britain by
Richard Clay (The Chaucer Press) Ltd,
Bungay, Suffolk*

CHAPTER ONE

LAURI felt restless rather than tired. The much rehearsed show at the Darnell School of Ballet had been performed that afternoon, and now she was on her way home to tell Aunt Pat all about it.

Aunt Pat had been in too much pain with her arthritis to be able to attend the performance, but it would please her to hear that all had gone well, and that Madame Darnell had invited a special guest to the show – the important Continental impresario, Signor Maxim di Corte.

All the pupils at the school knew why he had been invited and why he had come.

To see Julia Ray, the school's star performer, dance the role of Odette in the school's production of *Swan Lake*. Lauri had danced the role of Odile, the black swan.

She paused on the bridge beside the old mill, where in the spring there were real swans on the millpond. Today the trees along its banks were bare and stark, for winter still held sway over the countryside. Lauri loved the springtime, with the catkins long and crimson on the alders, golden on the weeping willows.

She gazed down into the darkening water and listened to the lonely twittering of a few birds. This way home to the cottage took longer, but she needed to unwind after the bustle and tension of the ballet. She had enjoyed dancing the role of Odile, but she knew as well as her fellow pupils that if Signor di Corte was on the lookout for a new dancer for his company, he would be bound to choose Julia. She was way ahead of the other girls in technique, and apart from that rather stunning to look at.

Lauri knew that she was not stunning. Even Aunt Pat, who had loved her and mothered her from an infant, had to admit that Lauri's charms were elusive.

Elusive, and disturbing. A quality that held the glimmers and shadows of beauty . . . the creation of it in movement. 'A reed through which all things blow into music.' Those words of Swinburne described Lauri, though she wasn't really aware of the fact.

In her own seventeen-year-old language, she was gawky as a cat, with the eyes of one.

Lauri's eyes were a dark topaz; her hair hung in a black, wind-blown tangle to her shoulder-blades. In the woods of Downhollow she was at one with the birds and squirrels; by the water running under this old stone bridge she was slim and quick as a fish, or a wind pattern on its surface. She was all spirit and very little substance. A wistful creature, fey with feeling. A wand in the hand of chance.

She stirred and came out of her daydream. It was growing late and Aunt Pat would begin to worry. So, hands plunged into the pockets of a corduroy jacket worn over trews that hugged her long legs, she turned in the direction of the cottage and began to race the wind.

Her aunt, Pat Donaldson, was a widow who had danced in a *corps de ballet* in her younger days, but she had never possessed that special quality that goes to make a ballerina. She had made a fairly good marriage, however, and been left comfortable enough to send Lauri to a first-class ballet school. She was ambitious for her niece, who didn't quite share those starry ambitions and was at present happy being a pupil of the dance.

The cottage stood with several others about half a mile from the village, and Lauri was greatly surprised to see a car parked in the kerb, midway between *their* gate and that of the people next door. She gave the gleaming black body of the car an intent look. Their neighbours had a rather classy visitor from the look of things, she thought, and went running along the path that led to the side door of the cottage.

'I'm home, Aunt Pat,' she carolled, finding the small kitchen empty.

'That's my niece now . . . Lauri.' Aunt Pat's voice lifted, coming from the parlour, a room they rarely used. 'Darling, come into the parlour!'

Said the spider to the fly, Lauri mentally tagged on, wondering who on earth Aunt Pat was entertaining in there. She went along the passage, hesitated a moment outside the door, then pushed it open and went in.

Cigar smoke and hot coffee mingled their aromas in the room. Aunt Pat sat in one armchair, Madame Darnell in another, while the smoker of the cigar rose from the settee as Lauri entered. He was impeccably clad in a dark grey suit, and he looked twenty times more intimidating here in this cottage parlour than he had looked in the hall of the ballet school, watching Madame's pupils perform *Swan Lake*.

'This is Signor di Corte, my child,' Madame was smiling, but in a rather tight-lipped way. 'He wishes to talk with you.'

'With me?' Lauri stood dumbfounded before the distinguished Venetian, who was Founder and Director of one of the world's finest ballet companies. Gods and muses! She felt a little weak as he appraised her from head to foot with dark eyes that seemed to see right through her. Magnetic eyes, deep-set in a lean haughty face dominated by a Roman nose. He was very erect and tall, a man whose force Lauri felt like a blow.

'You seem taken aback, Miss Garner.' His deep accented voice matched the well-bred assurance of his looks. 'May I ask the reason for your wide-eyed surprise?'

'Well – I hardly expected to come home and find you here, *signor*.' He had captured her gaze and she couldn't look away from him. She felt certain the drumming of her heart must be audible to him. 'I – I can't understand why you should want to talk to me.'

'You are too modest, *signorina* – please to sit down,' he gestured imperiously at the settee, and drew forward a chair for himself. He sat down facing her and crossed a long immaculately clad leg over the other. He lifted his cigar and drew on it, and all the time his eyes rested compelling and shrewd on Lauri's face, with its tri-angular eyes and high cheekbones. 'I wish to discuss your dancing,' he added.

'*My* dancing?' Lauri looked amazed. 'But we all thought at school that you were interested in Julia Ray – she danced so well.' Lauri glanced appealingly at her aunt, then at Madame. 'Julia is your star pupil, isn't she, Madame?'

'Signor di Corte does not seem to be in agreement with *my* view.' Madame Darnell shrugged and looked a trifle put out.

'Really?' Lauri couldn't help noticing that Aunt Pat was smiling as smugly as a tabby who had filched the cream from another cat's saucer.

She glanced back at Signor di Corte, who wasn't smiling at all. 'I am not interested in displays and pretty posturings,' he said curtly. 'Technical proficiency is not enough – for me. Tell me, Miss Garner, did you enjoy dancing the role of Odile?'

'Yes, *signor*,' she said quietly.

'Would you not have preferred the heroine role of Odette?'

'No.' She shook her head. 'I think it has less – character.'

'And less passion.' He regarded her for a long moment with those dark eyes that were so difficult to evade. 'I think you understand, for one so young, that with her body a dancer can express every emotion. Very possibly this is unconscious in you, but it is there, and it is something of far more value to a dancer than the ability to perform with exactitude the mere mechanics of the dance.'

Here he inclined his head half mockingly to Madame Darnell, and then he smiled, with such startling charm that Lauri all but caught her breath.

'A dancer is the sheath of a sword, a chalice holding fire and wine – Miss Garner,' his voice went from velvet to iron in a moment, 'why on-stage are you suddenly so nervous that you bungle the easiest of steps? Twice this afternoon I saw you falter – as though you trod on heated boards.'

Lauri stared at him, then suddenly as white as a sheet she sprang to her feet. 'Did you come here just to criticize me, *signor*?' she demanded.

'Lauri,' Madame Darnell looked scandalized, 'that is no way to speak to Signor di Corte. His advice is invaluable to a dance pupil.'

'My dear,' groaned Aunt Pat, 'Signor di Corte, you must excuse my niece – she's a rather highly strung girl – '

'Be composed, *signora*, I am well used to the tantrums and temperaments of dancers.' He scanned Lauri's white face with ice-dark eyes. '*Che e stato, signorina?*'

She knew he asked her a question, but she didn't understand Italian.

'I ask you what is the matter?' he said. 'I can see that it upsets you to give a poorer performance than you are capable of giving.'

'I – I have a lot more to learn, *signor*.' She thrust her hands into her pockets and braved his shrewd, penetrating eyes. 'Madame will tell you that.'

'Why, Lauri danced almost as soon as she could walk,' broke in Aunt Pat, proudly. 'Her parents were adagio dancers of great skill and on the stage themselves – '

'Please,' Lauri's eyes had gone dark with pain as she turned them to her aunt. 'I'm sure Signor di Corte has no interest in all that, and though I'm grateful to him for showing an interest in my dancing, you know, Aunt Pat, how I feel about the stage – '

'Surely you intend to turn professional?' he rapped out.

'My aunt wishes it.' Lauri gave him a frown and wished to goodness he would go and there could be peace again in the parlour. Right now it was crackling with an element that put her nerves on edge.

'And love is a great persuader, eh?' There was a hint of amusement in his voice. 'For love of your aunt you dance, though you dislike it.'

'To say I dislike dancing is putting it a bit strongly,' she protested. 'It isn't that I dislike dancing – '

'It is that you have a fear of the stage,' he said quietly.

She stiffened, and it flashed through her mind that he was frightening in his shrewdness. 'My parents died in a theatre fire when I was five,' she flared. 'Everyone says that children so young don't remember things, but I remember. I have nightmares about it – or more correctly stage frights. When I dance I remember, and that's why I don't want to go into professional ballet.'

The room fell quiet after her outburst. Aunt Pat's face was stricken. Madame Darnell looked uncomfortable. Signor di Corte rose to his feet and killed the butt of his cigar in a glass ashtray.

'It would be a great pity, *signorina*, to let what is past spoil your future,' he said in his deep voice with its tone of inflexibility. 'I did not come here this evening to offer criticism or encouragement to a pupil of the dance. I came because I wish you to become a member of my company. I thought I saw poetry and imagination in you. The will to be dedicated to the art, something I demand in all my dancers. Your line is clean and fresh, but if you have not the courage, or the desire to overcome what haunts you, then you are of little use to me.'

'Lauri,' Aunt Pat struggled to her feet and leant on her walking stick, 'you can't refuse such a wonderful offer. I won't let you!'

'Your niece must make up her own mind, *signora*. This must be her choice. Hers alone.' Signor di Corte pulled back his cuff and took a look at his watch. 'Right now I must be on my way back to London. I accompany my dancers to Wales, and then to Scotland. We will be gone three weeks. At the end of the month we will be back in London for a few days, and I will then contact you again, Miss Garner. In the meantime, will you think over my proposal?'

Lauri gazed back at him mutely. She felt him to be a man who could compel most people to do just what he wanted. His will was surely as unyielding as that straight back of his, yet in this moment she did not feel that he was compelling her to give in to him. He wished her to make up her own mind – and then again the world was full of promising dancers who lived only to dance.

He had his choice of the best.

'Don't ask yourself why *I* want you to become a member of my company,' he said, reading her mind. 'Ask yourself what *you* want, with courage and honesty. And remember that whatever happens to any of us in this life is not entirely due to chance, and that running away from a problem never helped to solve it.'

Having said this, he broke into the smile that was so startling. Lauri recalled the intense charm of it long after he and Madame Darnell had left the cottage and driven away in his black car. The man was unforgettable, and in the days that followed he and the things he had said were constantly in her thoughts.

'You can't turn down his offer,' Aunt Pat reiterated. 'My dear, another like it might never come your way again. The di Corte Ballet Company is world renowned. It's an honour to be asked to join dancers like Lydia Andreya and Michael Lonza.'

It was evening time, and Lauri was sprawled like a supple young cat on the carpet in front of the kitchen fire. Aunt Pat sat in her favourite chair, a rocker with a cushioned back.

'Lonza,' Lauri murmured. 'The Panther. It must be quite an experience to see him dance.'

'You have the chance to work in the same company with him,' her aunt said explosively. 'To know him, perhaps to dance with him.'

Lauri broke into laughter. 'Darling, I would be a very minor member of the *corps de ballet*. Lonza is something unique. The best judges of male dancing consider him to be potentially great, a "god of the dance" as they call it. Six years ago Maxim di Corte saw him dancing flamenco among the gipsies of Madrid, sent him to ballet school and then offered him a contract.'

'Just as Signor di Corte is offering you one.' Aunt Pat gazed down at Lauri with puzzled eyes. 'It would be a dream come true for most dancers, but you call it a nightmare – to the man's face!'

'He didn't like that, did he?' Lauri cradled her knees and gazed into the fire. 'His eyes burned like anthracite. Aunt Pat, his standards are as high as the stars! Where would someone like me fit in? What would I be – a bondmaid?'

'You do say the oddest things, my dear.' Aunt Pat studied the face of her niece-child in the fire glow; sensitive, angular, the unawakened lips touched by pain. 'In my youthful days I would have given my front teeth for a quarter of your talent – yes, pull a face and look scornful, but do you think a man like Maxim di Corte would have put himself out to come here and talk to you if he hadn't seen something special in you? It put Madame Darnell's nose out of joint. He obviously didn't want her dancing Ray of sunshine.'

Lauri smiled a little. 'They all know at the school that he came here. They all think he must be round the bend to want me in preference to Julia. Look how pretty she is!'

'You, my gawky little cat, have the talent,' Aunt Pat said with relish. 'Signor di Corte called it poetry and imagination, and to be able to convey those in motion is the true essence of ballet dancing. Otherwise, as he said, the dancer performs a mere succession of pretty posturings. Oh, come on, Lauri, you know he's right! The ability to dance is in your bones – it's your morbid fear of theatres and dancing on a stage that is making you hold back.'

'Yes,' Lauri admitted with a shudder. 'I like being a pupil of the dance. I could never face up to being a professional performer. I'm sorry, Aunt Pat. I know how much you want it, but when I get on to a stage I do make silly blunders. I – I lose confidence.'

'You're a funny one.' Aunt Pat stroked the dark head near her knees. 'Do you think your parents would want you to go on like this? They were real professionals. The show came first.'

'And it killed them,' Lauri said huskily. 'I heard the fire bells – our lodgings were just across the road from the theatre, and those bells, dozens of them, have never stopped clamouring in my head.'

'They'll stop clamouring the first time a real audience storms you with applause. Don't you want that, Lauri? Achievement, heaven's second most elusive star.'

'What is the first?' Lauri asked with a smile.

'The happiness brought by love, my dear.'

'Is it so elusive?' Lauri raised her dusky-gold eyes to her aunt's face. 'You found it, didn't you?'

'I found security,' her aunt said quietly. 'I was over thirty when I married Stanley, and by then I knew I should never get beyond the ranks of the *corps de ballet*. He was kind to me. It was nice to be cosy and cared for.'

Nice and cosy, Lauri thought. A steady warmth, but never a flame that burned up and up, over your whole body – she shuddered at the way those flames crept into all her thinking.

'Dear Aunt Pat,' she said, 'how could I leave you, anyway? How could I go away?'

'To let you go, my little winged cat, would be a wrench for me, but I wouldn't dream of stopping you. Think how it will develop you as a dancer and a person to travel abroad. Lauri, you *must* accept Signor di

Corte's offer. He said he'd get in contact with you again at the end of the month.'

'He'll probably forget,' Lauri said half-hopefully.

'Lauri, you brat!' Aunt Pat shook her niece's shoulder. 'He isn't a man who changes his mind once he has made it up. Didn't you notice his chin?'

'Yes, solid obstinacy,' Lauri laughed. With a dent right in the centre of it, she remembered vividly, as she leant forward and threw another piece of wood on the fire.

She was at the *barre* next day at ballet school when Julia Ray came up to her. Julia was a pretty girl, but her mouth at the moment was sulky. 'Even if Signor di Corte had asked me to join his company,' she said, 'my father wouldn't have let me. He says I'm to join an English company. Margot Fonteyn is English, after all.'

'She's marvellous,' Lauri smiled. 'Anyway, I'm not sure yet what I'm going to do. Nothing is definitely fixed up.'

'I see.' Julia ran her blue eyes over Lauri's thin, sensitive face. 'I should imagine you'd feel out of place among all those exotic foreign dancers. They stay in an old palace in Venice when their ballet season is over, and you can bet it's terribly run down and damp.'

Lauri extended a long leg and bent her head towards it. 'I expect the *palazzo* is a bit run down,' she said, 'but I should imagine it's a romantic old place. From all accounts the di Corte family have lived in it for centuries.'

'You could hardly take your aunt with you, Lauri.' There was a note of smug satisfaction in Julia's voice. 'She couldn't stand all that dampness with her complaint.'

Lauri had already thought of this, and it was foremost

among her reasons for not wanting to join the di Corte Company.

The end of the month drew near, and once again Aunt Pat pressed her to make up her mind. 'Signor di Corte isn't a man to be played around with,' she added.

'I know,' Lauri said. 'But I can't picture myself in real ballet.'

'It's like being a member of a rather special family.' Aunt Pat spoke from her own knowledge of the ballet company to which she had belonged in her youth. 'The people of the ballet world have a quality that can't really be put into words. They're unique, dedicated, not quite of this earth. I'm sure you'd fit in, Lauri.'

'I feel that I'd be lost among them like a Jenny-wren among a group of jays.' Lauri's laughter had an edge of apprehension to it. 'Look at the Maestro himself.'

'Did you find Signor di Corte unnerving?' Aunt Pat's casualness of voice didn't quite match her sharpness of eye as she glanced down at her niece.

'He was a trifle overwhelming,' Lauri admitted. 'I – I sensed something *ruthless* about him. He moulds people to his tastes, and he makes them submit whether they want to or not.'

'Very probably.' Aunt Pat spoke dryly. 'Ballet is not an art that can be daubed in bright colours and splashes on a canvas. It has to be staged, and the result has to be a perfect blending of tones, shapes and movements. The dancer is the clay of this art, and out of the raw material of supple but unsophisticated bodies Signor di Corte shapes his dancers until they fit into the classic frame of the true ballet.' Aunt Pat drew hard on her cigarette.

'It's quite a job, Lauri, being the artistic director of

a ballet company. A brilliant knowledge of all the arts is essential, along with a fertile business brain, the ability to inspire the artists who work for him, and the driving force and charm that finds the patronage which keeps an independent company off the rocks.'

'The iron hand in the velvet gauntlet,' Lauri said flippantly. 'You sound as though you were quite taken with the man.'

'I thought he looked supremely capable of doing a hard job well, but I suppose to a youngster like you, he would seem very worldly.'

'I'm not that young,' Lauri protested.

'My dear, you can be wise beyond your years,' Aunt Pat agreed fondly. 'But you will admit that there are times when you behave like a gamine who won't grow up, nor do you seem to care for boys very much. You never bring any home to tea.'

'Boys are all right to dance with,' Lauri said carelessly. 'Apart from the classroom, I find them boring.'

'The men you meet in the di Corte Company will not be schoolboys,' Aunt Pat said meaningly. 'Dare I hope that you can cope, chicken?'

'My decision about joining the di Corte Company lies with the gods and muses.' Lauri leapt to her feet in one supple movement. 'Now I'm going to make our cocoa. Um, I think I'll have a cold meat sandwich with it. How about you?'

'Not this time of the night! I'd never get to sleep.' Aunt Pat rocked lazily and watched her young niece carving meat off the cold Sunday roast and popping pieces into her mouth. The girl was thin as a wand, with slim, arched feet that were invariably slipperless. Her black hair was carelessly tied back with a ribbon, and the lines of her figure were barely discernible.

A beloved enigma to Pat Donaldson. Dear as a daughter. Full of talent and nerves. Part dreamer, part gamine, with a bit of angel thrown in.

They had supper, then made their way up to bed. As they paused on the landing, Aunt Pat touched Lauri's cheek coaxingly. 'When the time comes for you to decide about your future, little cat, remember what Signor di Corte said to you. That it would be a pity, my dear, to let the sad past spoil what lies ahead for you.'

'I'll remember,' Lauri kissed her aunt goodnight, and entered her little cottage bedroom with its ceiling braced by old dark beams, its white quilt covering the single bed, and red hooked rugs.

She glanced round the white-painted walls, adorned with ballet pictures cut out of magazines and programmes. She knelt on her bed and studied a big black and white photograph of Michael Lonza holding the lovely ballerina Andreya above his head in a pose from the Black Swan *pas de deux*. Lauri smiled as she thought of herself in the school show, dancing the role of Odile with a callow boy.

What, she wondered, did it feel like to dance with a man like Lonza – the Panther, as critics and balletomanes called him? He was darkly handsome, with the eyes and cheekbones of a Tartar.

In the terrible days of the Russian revolution his father – someone at Court – had managed to escape into Rumania, where he had been sheltered and loved by a gipsy dancer. Then they had drifted apart, and when she died her son Michael had roamed all over Europe.

He looked a pagan with a sense of humour, Lauri thought. She had no doubts about his gifts as a performer, and wished she could see him dance.

CHAPTER TWO

An air of expectation hung about the cottage at Down-hollow, and then midway through the last week of the month Lauri arrived home from ballet school to find a letter awaiting her.

'Open it before I go quietly crazy!' Aunt Pat exclaimed.

'I'm scared.' Lauri stood fiddling with the envelope, which bore a London postmark.

'What about?' her aunt derided her. 'I'm sure you'll be relieved if Signor di Corte has written to say he has changed his mind about wanting you in his ballet company.'

'Do you think he has?' Lauri wouldn't have believed that her heart could sink so low.

'Well, there's only one way to find out.' Aunt Pat took the letter out of Lauri's hand, ripped open the envelope and drew out a single typewritten page. She scanned it, then broke into a smile.

'He wants you to meet him in London,' she said excitedly. 'He writes. . . .'

'Let me see.' Lauri bent over the letter with her aunt, and her heart beat rapidly as she read that Signor di Corte wished to pursue their conversation of the sixth of that month, and as members of his company were dancing in a gala ballet at the Covent Garden Opera House on Saturday evening, he thought she might like to see the performance. If she could manage to come to London on Saturday, he would be pleased if she would meet him in the foyer of the Strand Palace Hotel at seven-thirty.

'You'll go, of course?' Aunt Pat spoke breathlessly. 'A gala at Covent Garden – Lonza is bound to be dancing, and you've been longing to see him.'

'Yes,' Lauri's eyes were wide and startled, 'isn't it strange?'

'Strange is hardly the word, my girl. Now you're going to need a new dress, so I suggest we go up to London on Friday and buy it there. It will hardly be worth our while coming home again, so we'll stay at a hotel for the weekend.'

'A whole weekend in London would be fun,' Lauri agreed. 'It will make a nice break for you, Aunt Pat, and perhaps Signor di Corte will have another ticket to spare – '

'Lauri,' Aunt Pat broke in dryly, 'I'm not the sort who tags along on a girl's first big date.'

'Date?' Lauri echoed. 'This is strictly business, and you love going to the ballet as much as I do.'

'I know more about life than you do, my pet.' Aunt Pat regarded her niece with a sudden twinkle in her eye. 'Even when a man only wants to talk business with a girl, he doesn't want her aunt there holding her hand. You'll have to get over the shyness he might arouse in you. He's only a man, after all, and most of them are a lot kinder than women are.'

'I don't think he looked particularly kind,' Lauri said, remembering the strength in his features, and the piercing quality of his eyes. One look and you knew him to be a man who had known palaces and boulevards; beautiful women and strange cities.

Lauri and her aunt went up to London on the Friday morning. After lunching at their hotel in Russell Square, they drove in a taxi to a smart shop in Connaught

Street, where they looked at evening dresses and finally chose a maize-gold dress with a youthful neckline.

'A fur jacket would really set that dress off.' Aunt Pat turned to the assistant. 'We can't run to the real thing, but have you anything young-looking in lapin?' she asked.

The assistant went away to have a look, while Lauri protested that she could wear her best coat over the dress. 'Signor di Corte knows we aren't rolling in money,' she said. 'He won't expect me to turn up dressed like a deb.'

'He's a sophisticated man and I don't suppose he'll want you to look suburban in a coat over an evening dress', Aunt Pat rejoined. 'You funny child, don't you want to look nice for such an attractive man?'

'He thinks me little more than a child,' Lauri grinned. 'I'm not being taken to the Opera House on the strength of my glamour – he wants me to see some of his dancers in action.'

Lauri's eyes glistened at the thought. Michael Lonza was dancing *L'Après-midi d'un Faune*, and having read all about the ballet's creator, the tragic Nijinsky, she couldn't wait to see a performance of the ballet.

To Aunt Pat's delight the assistant returned with a short lapin jacket which fitted Lauri snugly, the collar a soft brown frame about her pointed face and large enquiring eyes.

'I look more like a cat than a glamour puss,' she commented.

'Cats have "it", my child.' Aunt Pat leaned on her stick and surveyed her niece like a genial witch. 'You'll do, when you're all dressed up, with your hair braided round the crown of your head.'

Upon their return to the hotel, Aunt Pat had a cup

of tea and left Lauri to amuse herself for a couple of hours. She went out again, and on impulse jumped on a bus that took her to the end of the Strand. From there she walked up Drury Lane to Covent Garden Market, where she stood in front of the Opera House and felt like doing a pirouette at the thought of tomorrow evening.

Whatever the outcome of her talk with Signor di Corte, she was sure of seeing some fabulous dancing. A gala excitement would light up this square . . . there would be that special magic in the air which ballet dancers seemed to create.

The maize-gold dress echoed the lights in Lauri's eyes, and her hair hung in a thick, glossy braid down over her bare left shoulder.

'You would look at least a couple of years older with your hair up,' Aunt Pat coaxed.

'It makes my neck look like Swanilda's', Lauri laughed nervously. She was unused to dressing up, and made rather shy by her own reflection in the mirror. The dress gave her a lissom look, while her shoulders and neck had a whiteness she had not noticed before. From the lobes of her ears bobbed a pair of small topazes.

Aunt Pat held the lapin jacket and Lauri slipped into it. Their eyes met in the mirror. 'Enjoy every moment of this evening, Lauri,' her aunt said gently. 'And be sure you make the right decision when Signor di Corte asks you again to join his company. He will, my dear, because he knows a born dancer when he sees one . . . and he has a very obstinate chin.'

Lauri's fingers clenched on her theatre purse, then she smiled and kissed her aunt on the cheek.

'Now have you got everything?' Aunt Pat eyed her niece with pride and a touch of anxiety. 'What about your taxi fare? You can't ride to the Strand Palace in a bus.'

'And there isn't a pumpkin in sight for you to wave your wand over,' Lauri grinned. 'I have a five-pound note in my purse, so I promise to ride in style to meet Prince Alarming!'

As her taxi turned into Kingsway, Lauri could feel her nerves tightening up. They sped past the neon-lighted shops and the people thronging the pavements. The smell of London came in through the open window, but its noise could not drown the clamour of her heart-beats.

All too soon for Lauri the taxi arrived at the Strand Palace, and her knees felt weak under the long silk skirt of her dress as she paid the fare. She turned to survey the hotel with its look of discreet opulence and its uniformed doorman, then trying to look as though she entered such places every day of her life, Lauri made her way into the foyer with its marbled columns and chandeliers.

She glanced about her for a tall individual with a head like a Roman conqueror, but saw only a few ordinary mortals. She swallowed nervously, and then stood delving into her purse for something to do. It wasn't that she was the only person waiting here for someone, but she felt conspicuous because she was so unused to wearing a silk evening dress and a fur jacket. Despite their sophistication, she was sure she looked as gauche as she was feeling.

All at once Lauri tensed. She glanced up and saw a tall figure in a dark evening suit approaching her. A nerve fluttered in Lauri's throat, and she was forcing her lips into a smile when he reached her. 'We meet again, Miss Garner,' he held out a hand, into which she put hers rather timidly. 'I am glad you could come to Covent Garden with me tonight – I had an idea that if I held out some ballet as a bait, you would rise to it.'

His dark eyes glimmered with humour as they held hers. 'How is your aunt?' he asked, releasing her hand. 'I believe she was not too well the last time we met?'

'We came up to London together,' Lauri told him. 'Aunt Pat is a lot better than she was – it's awful that she should suffer with arthritis after being so active in her younger days. She was in ballet, you know.'

'Yes, I was most interested to hear that.' His gaze was shrewd as it dwelt on Lauri. 'We have a little time to spare before we go to the Opera House, so would you like to come into the cocktail lounge and have a drink?'

She nodded, and felt his arm brush her waist as he piloted her into the softly-lit lounge with its low tables and deep armchairs. They sat down facing each other and he beckoned a waiter to their table.

'What will you have to drink, Miss Garner?' he asked.

'I'll have a Green Goddess, please.' Lauri was determined to show him that she wasn't as unworldly as she looked.

He quirked an eyebrow at her request, then turned blandly to the waiter and asked for one Green Goddess, and a gin and Italian.

'Do you go often to the ballet, Miss Garner?' He opened his cigarette case but did not offer it to her. She was a dancer, of course, and not to be encouraged to smoke!

'As often as possible, *signor*.' She found herself watching his lean hands as he lit his cigarette. 'A few months ago Aunt Pat and I went to see Makarova dance *Giselle*. I queued for hours for the tickets, but I love listening to the balletomanes discussing their favourite dancers.'

'Did you enjoy the ballet?' He sat back in his chair and gazed at her with disconcerting directness through his cigarette smoke.

'Every second of it,' she said warmly. 'Aunt Pat is an intense fan of Margot Fonteyn's and she thinks her *Giselle* the greatest.'

'It is a strange, haunting ballet and was very much suited to the personality of Margot Fonteyn, he agreed. 'We have it in our repertoire, but the role is inclined to disturb Andreya – you will be seeing Andreya dance this evening.'

'I'm looking forward to it.' Lauri's eyes glistened. 'I've wanted for a long time to see Michael Lonza dance. Is he as remarkable as the ballet critics say, *signor*?'

'One day soon he will take his place beside the greatest male dancers in the world.' Maxim di Corte glanced at the cigarette in his fingers. 'How would you like to dance with him, Miss Garner?'

'Golly, it's something I can't even imagine.' She gave a laugh. 'I shall never be in his class.'

'You are remarkably modest for a female.' The Venetian had an alarming fascination when he smiled. 'But let me assure you that I would not bother with a dancer unless I thought that she had talent – ah, here come our drinks.'

As he paid the waiter for them, Lauri studied him under the fan of her lashes. Her heart still beat quickly from the effects of his smile and what he had just said about her dancing talent. It had to be true, for no man as distinguished as this one would bother with a girl like herself unless she had *real* ability.

She felt the pull of the man; descendant of a *condottiere*, and the grandson of Travilla, who had been one of the world's most magical ballerinas.

'*Saluta*,' he said as she picked up her Green Goddess and they drank in unison.

'Of what are you thinking, *signorina*?' he asked suddenly.

'I – I couldn't possibly tell you, *signor*.' She took a hasty sip at her drink, a cocktail she liked because of its fascinating name.

'I insist that you do.' His gaze compelled her to look at him. 'I think you have made a judgment about me, and I wish to hear what it is so that I can defend myself.'

She smiled, amused by the idea of Maxim di Corte having to defend himself against Lauri Garner.

'I think you could be quite without mercy in quest of what you want,' she said bravely. 'I have read about the *condottiere* in your background.'

'Really?' His eyes dwelt for a moment on the glossy braid hanging down over her shoulder. 'May I point out that gentler men than I have said that a "cherished grief is an iron chain". It may well hurt you to dance in a theatre because of the way your parents died, but it will kill you in your soul if you don't dance.'

'Oh –' pain seemed to grab at her throat, 'why did you come to the Darnell School and pick on me?'

'I might so easily not have noticed you,' he said frankly. 'On your final exit in the ballet, what caught my eye was the way in which you *melted* from the stage. One moment you were there, and then you were gone – like the little witch-bird. The other girl, the one Madame wished me to notice,' he spoke impatiently, 'she was too annoyingly aware of her own charms and her audience. It is death to a role for the dancer to be more aware of herself than the character she plays. Not all the technique in the world could excuse such egoism, least of all in a mere pupil of the dance. It is humility that makes great artistes.'

He had spoken forcibly, from his heart, Lauri felt sure, as much as from his great knowledge of the art of ballet. The spirit of the dance was in his blood, implanted there by his famous grandmother.

'Is it not the wish of your heart to be a dancer?' he murmured.

Her lashes trembled, then veiled her dusky-gold eyes as she felt the pull of this man on the dancer within her.

'I see, you have not the kidney for what I demand of you,' now he mocked her. 'You feel safe here in England, clinging to the skirts of your aunt. That you may have the gift for making a great many people forget themselves and their worries is of no real concern to you. You are going to keep it to yourself, eh?'

She flinched at his gift for knowing exactly where to strike and hurt the most. 'If I failed to come up to your standards, you would soon send me packing,' she said warmly.

'And you would sooner not take that chance?' he drawled. 'Come, are you going through life afraid all the time to take chances? If so, you will never find any true happiness or satisfaction.'

His dark eyes wickedly mocked her. His shoulders were square and strong under the dark material of his tuxèdo; his proud head and Roman features merged into a hard throat, tawny against white linen and taut black tie. In his buttonhole there was a small red carnation, a touch of the exotic that quickened the beat of her heart.

How on earth did a mere girl fight so determined a man? Lauri wondered. Couldn't he see that she would be no use in a theatre, dancing for other people?

Suddenly she gave a start for he had reached across the table and taken hold of her hand. 'All dancers are a little like children,' he said quietly. 'I watch out for the well-being of mine, as much as for their careers – I am not, you know, a Svengali with a troupe of Trilbys.'

She gave a nervous little laugh, for that was exactly how she did think of him.

'I don't ask the impossible of my dancers, but it is amazing how close they come at times to achieving it.' His eyes held hers. 'My company has been travelling and dancing for several months now, and performing many ballets – but on Wednesday of next week we set sail for my *palazzo* in Venice.'

'You sail on – Wednesday?' Lauri exclaimed.

'What is the matter, Miss Garner?' His eyes were mesmeric. 'Did you imagine I would give you a few more weeks in which to dither about joining us? I have already allowed you three, and tonight you must give me your final answer.'

'But I can't.' There was a touch of anguish about her face. 'There's my aunt to consider – '

'Please,' his fingers tightened about hers, 'don't make the Signora Donaldson your excuse. She knows that separation from you is unavoidable if you choose to join my company, and she will not stand in your way. That is what a dancing career teaches one, *signorina*, unselfishness and a unique quality of kindness. How old are you exactly, Miss Garner?'

'I – I shall be eighteen in July,' she faltered.

'Old enough to start being a *divetta*.' His smile was very worldly in that moment. 'You have never been to Venice, eh?'

'Aunt Pat finds it increasingly difficult to get about, but we managed a holiday in Holland last year,' Lauri told him. 'I loved the canals, and the old Rembrandt houses.'

'Venice is a feminine city, lovely as her name – and now, *signorina*,' he let go of her hand and rose to his feet, 'we go to the ballet.'

A rose-glow spread from behind the proscenium curtains as they began to rise and the house lights to go down. The conductor tapped his baton, there was a sound of woodwinds and flutes, and the gauzy inner curtains slowly lifted on a forest scene. Lightly clad nymphs ran across the stage, their veils changing colour as they danced . . . then there came a sudden dramatic change in the music. A lean figure was sculptured in the air as he leapt from among the trees, and a palpable stir of excitement ran through the Opera House.

Lonza in pursuit of the nymphs, seeming to travel in space like a jungle creature after its prey; supple, pantherine, his swarthy skin taking on the sheen of bronze in the changing lights.

Lauri knew that such exciting elevation was due to the steely strength in Lonza's legs and back, but only someone with a deep love of the dance could have communicated as he did with every sinew and heartbeat, every gleam of the oblique eyes above the Tartar cheekbones.

That ten-minute ballet was over all too soon for Lauri, then a storm of applause was sweeping the huge auditorium and the tiers of seats and boxes. Lonza stood alone on the vast stage, his head bowed, lean as a boy, until at last he was lost behind the curtains and an audible sigh escaped from a thousand female throats.

Lauri had sat stage-struck and enchanted . . . but never fully forgetful of her companion. Now she turned to look at him and saw that he was looking at her. 'At last you have seen Lonza dance,' he murmured.

'He's superb.' Her eyes shone into Maxim di Corte's dark ones. 'To remain suspended in the air as long as he did – it's hardly human!'

'I assure you he is very human.' There was something sardonic about Maxim di Corte's smile as he sat back in the shadows of the box they were sharing.

Each moment of that gala evening was enchanted for Lauri, and she felt the quickening beat of her heart as the time drew near for Lonza to dance again, this time with Lydia Andreya.

Maxim di Corte slipped away just before the stars of his company were due to appear, and Lauri sat alone amidst the glamour of the Opera House and the gala audience. She knew that people in the other boxes were looking at her and wondering who she was. She felt their inquisitive eyes upon her long braid of hair, her topaz eardrops, and the slim pallor of her neck above the scooped top of her dress. Her hands clenched together in her lap and she wished Signor di Corte would hurry back to shield her with his cool aloofness.

Suddenly she heard a woman say clearly : 'Do you suppose he's getting tired of Andreya? She still looks stunning on-stage, but she is beginning to show her age off-stage – then there's that husband of hers.'

Lauri stared at one of the gilt mermaids decorating the circle of seats nearest to her. Like every ballet fan, she knew that Andreya was parted from her husband, but it shook her to learn that Maxim di Corte had gone backstage for a personal reason rather than a supervisory one.

A feeling of relief overtook her as the house lights began to dim and to conceal her from the curious occupants of the nearby boxes. The great curtains were opening, lifting on magic. Sea-purple shimmers played over rocks and the stark rigging and broken timbers of a wrecked ship. There were strange trees hung with sea-fruit, and sea-nymphs performed a garland dance with seaweeds, encircling a huge anemone whose tendrils slowly opened. Out of it rose Andreya as a sea-enchantress, her hair a dusky veil about a curiously exciting face as she ran on *pointe* to the wrecked ship and drew out of it with enticing movements of her hands the drowned yet alive body of the young seaman she had enchanted.

A tingle of excitement ran through Lauri, and she was conscious for a brief moment of a hand touching hers as Signor di Corte took the seat beside her . . . she smiled without looking at him, spellbound by the scene upon the stage. It was one of strange allure, the man drawn hither and thither by the white hand of Andreya, embracing and caressing at her sinister behest.

They danced together brilliantly, and it didn't seem to matter that Lonza looked at times a boy beside Andreya. The dance called also for high, sweeping lifts which he must have found strenuous. Andreya was tall for a ballerina, but Lonza showed no sign of stress. His muscles seemed of steel and he made his partner look as light as a leaf and superbly steady when she performed her pirouettes.

Lauri couldn't drag her gaze from the stage, yet she felt the intensity of the man at her side. She sensed that his dark eyes were following Andreya's every movement.

The action on-stage grew even more dramatic as the enchanted seaman suddenly threw a noose of seaweeds about the throat of his terrible mistress and tried to choke her. But she was an enchantress who could not be killed, and her laughter rang out mockingly as the great curtains swept together and the last notes of the music echoed her laughter.

There was silence for a moment, like a held breath, then a storm of clapping broke out and the curtains parted again to reveal the *corps de ballet* in their coral colours. Then Lonza placed an arm about Andreya's waist and brought her forward, and as she sank to the stage among the flowers that were raining down he stepped back a few paces and watched his partner receiving the homage of the crowd. At last she threw him a glance of appeal – as though it were all a little too much for her – and when he came forward and kissed her hand, the applause mounted to a crescendo.

Andreya and Lonza had danced away with the honours of the evening, and a flushed and excited Lauri was clapping with everyone else, giving two unique performers an ovation.

'*Signor*,' Lauri's eyes were alight with pleasure as they met his, 'how proud you must feel of those two.'

'Of course.' He smiled down at her. 'Would you like to meet them?'

'Do you mean it?' Her eyes seemed to fill her face.

'I always mean what I say,' he said dryly. 'There is to be a farewell party at the Strand Palace, and I don't think another hour of excitement will hurt you – child though you look.'

'I'm not a child,' she protested, but he merely laughed as he adjusted her fur jacket about her shoulders, and after making sure that she was leaving none of her belongings behind in her excitement he began to pilot her towards an exit.

At the exit they were halted by a group of people who urged that he and his company remain in England a while longer. 'My dancers need a holiday and I am taking them home to Venice,' he protested laughingly. '*Grazie*, you are all more than kind to want us to return. We will, I promise you. . . .'

At last he and Lauri managed to escape into the chilly night air of Covent Garden. They pushed their way through a throng of fans waiting with autograph-books, into the square. He glanced about for a taxi, but they had all been taken and their rear lights blinked in the darkness as they drove off.

'You will catch cold if we wait about here for a cab,' he said. 'It will take us only a few minutes to walk down to the Strand.'

'A walk will help clear my head,' she laughed. 'Oh, what an evening, *signor*. I shall never forget it.'

'It is not yet over, *signorina*.' His voice sounded extra deep and significant in the darkness, and with a cool but kindly brusqueness he drew her nearer to him as they walked towards the Strand. Close to him like this, Lauri was very aware of how tall he was, and how distinguished in his evening wear.

Suddenly she remembered why she was with him . . . tonight she must promise or refuse to dance for him.

'I – I love the night time.' She hastened into words because her thoughts were too disturbing. 'Especially on the Downs at home, when the stars come out and make a ballet of their own.'

'Dancers are nocturnal creatures,' he said. 'They light

up in a subtle way when dusk falls, like the exotic moths
one sees out in the tropics.'

'Have you and your company been all over the world,
signor?' she asked.

'We have been to a good many places,' and he told
her about the magnificent stage of the Bolshoi Theatre,
which enabled the ballerinas and their partners to make
remarkable runs and leaps. 'One is told constantly out
there that the Bolshoi lacks the glamour of the old
Imperial days,' he added, 'but it is a great experience
to see *Petrushka* performed in a real Russian setting.'

He was talking about Japanese dancing at the Kabuki
Theatre in Tokyo as they turned into the Strand and
the neon lights played over his face. 'What do you
think of London, *signor*?' Lauri asked impulsively.

'I find it a stimulating city, but naturally I make
comparisons with my *Venezia benedetta*.' A smile
grooved deeper the lines of authority in his face. 'It is,
my Venice, a city like a masked beauty. Always there
is the splash of water against old grey stone, the creak
and sway of moored gondolas, and old *palazzos* mirrored
in the lagoon. It is Byron's "fairy city of the heart". A
priceless mural centuries old – ah, but I could go on
talking about Venice all night, and we have something
else to discuss.'

Her heart skipped a beat, and she felt his lean hand
under her elbow as he guided her across the road. The
hand of the Maestro, which set the di Corte dancers
spinning and leaping and running across the stages of
the world.

'Do you imagine,' he pushed open the swing doors
of the Strand Palace and she was whisked in under the
blaze of chandeliers, 'that you can defy destiny, the
dictates of your own heart – and me?'

Had she imagined she could escape him? Even as she wondered, she was being led into the brightly lit ballroom where the farewell party was being held for him and his ballet company.

'Come, choose now,' he said, and he awaited his answer even as a waiter approached with champagne and people turned from the buffet to watch them as they faced each other under the sparkle of a chandelier. She raised her eyes to meet his . . . feeling as helpless as a lamb plucked off the downs by an eagle. 'Have I a choice?' she murmured. 'What will you do with me if I join your company and then fail you?'

'I shall throw you into the dungeons below my *palazzo*,' he said dryly. He turned and took two glasses of champagne off the tray of the hovering waiter. He placed one of the brimming glasses in her hand. 'Drink every drop of that, and then I will introduce you to everyone and satisfy their burning curiosity about you,' he added.

She became at once conscious of the people watching them. There was a woman draped in white fox, and Lauri recognized her as the person who from a nearby box at the Opera House had speculated aloud on Maxim di Corte's devotion to Lydia Andreya. . . .

Andreya came sweeping into the ballroom at that moment, dramatically gowned and carrying an immense bouquet of golden roses. Her dark red hair was drawn back from a face like a worn but radiant carving. 'Maxim!' she cried, and came towards him.

He stepped forward at once to meet his *prima ballerina* with an outstretched hand. 'My dear Lydia,' he smiled, 'come and meet the little girl I was telling you about – Lauri Garner. She sails with us on Wednesday to Venice.'

Lauri was gazing wide-eyed at Andreya, but when Maxim di Corte said so firmly that she was sailing with them on Wednesday, she glanced at him with a protest on her lips that was never uttered. His commanding eyes captured hers, robbing her of the will to do anything but submit to him. Such dark eyes, set in the Roman face that was like no other she had ever seen. As he held her gaze, and others watched them, she knew herself caught up in one of those fateful moments from which there was no retreat.

'So you sail with us on Wednesday, eh?'

'Yes –' Lauri heard her own reply with a sense of disbelief, and pulse-racing wonderment. 'Yes, Madame Andreya.'

The ballerina swept her brilliant gaze over Lauri's face, from which apprehension and excitement had taken all the colour, leaving her dusky-gold eyes and winged eyebrows to stand out in relief. 'Welcome to our ranks, Miss Garner,' drawled the ballerina. 'I hope you realize that hard work and discipline are our main rewards for giving ourselves into the power of this Venetian autocrat.'

'Lydia,' he laughed, 'you will frighten the child.'

'Oh dear,' the ballerina took a glass of champagne and smiled mockingly. 'Is she one of the nervous sort?'

Lauri, all nerves, wanted to turn in that moment and bolt from the ballroom. Maxim di Corte must have noticed the desperate glance which she cast towards the exit, for in an instant his long fingers were holding her by the wrist. 'Come to the buffet and have some caviare,' he said. 'Young people are always hungry, unless you are one of those who subsists on milk and a lettuce leaf?'

'*Signor –*'

'Yes, *signorina*?' His dark eyes dwelt enigmatically on her upraised young face, the topaz drops glinting in her ears against her long braid of hair and slim, pale neck.

'I – I've never had caviare,' she said huskily, defeated by something within herself that could not fight the compelling personality of Maxim di Corte. The man who would in a few short days carry her off to his palace in Venice.

CHAPTER THREE

THE sea trip to Venice was a time of relaxation for most members of the ballet company, but Lauri couldn't help feeling sad about leaving Aunt Pat. They had been together ever since Lauri was five, and she missed already her aunt's company and counsel. Now she had to stand on her own feet. The dancing feet which had loved to roam over the Downs at home, and were feeling right now the deck of a ship under them as she took a solitary stroll before turning in for the night.

She was sharing a cabin with a couple of dancers named Concha and Viola. They were members of the *corps de ballet*, and such a lively, pretty pair that most of their time was taken up by their admirers. In consequence of this Lauri, who was shy, was left to wander about the ship on her own.

She saw very little of Maxim di Corte, who seemed to spend most of his time with Andreya, and Bruno Lanning, the company's régisseur. These three did not join in any of the deck games, and the concerts appeared to bore them. Slim and sleek in a fur coat, Andreya would promenade between the two men, or scintillate at the Captain's table, while Maxim di Corte listened and smiled in his grave, dark-eyed way.

Lauri paused beside the rail of the deck on which she was taking her stroll. The moon was up and the ocean glimmered. The ship drew nearer all the time to Venice – bride of the Adriatic – and she felt tonight a stirring of interest in the city that had grown up on many small islands to become a place loved throughout its history by poets like Byron and Browning, and cavaliers like Casanova.

Her gaze followed the moon, and she thought of the Venetian poem which likened the first gondola to a crescent moon, dropped out of the sky to provide shelter for a pair of eloping lovers. Lauri enjoyed old stories and legends and Venice was probably full of them. She began to feel more eager to see the city, where the ballet company was to reside for a couple of months at the *palazzo* which had been in Maxim di Corte's family for centuries.

He was the last male member of his family. And it was plain that he was as proud and shrewd and able to command as the Venetians of long ago, whose efforts had made their city so beautiful and famous. His line was an old one and he would have to marry to ensure its continuation. Lauri thought of Andreya, with her strange, striking face . . . and the husband she already had.

Again, as Lauri stood at the ship's rail, she became aware of the tangy, drifting aroma of a cigarette. She half-turned and saw the outline of a long, lean shape in one of the steamer-chairs behind her. Though the smoker's face was masked by the shadows, the scent of his cigarette gave him away to Lauri.

'You look very lonely in the moonlight, Nijinka,' he drawled. 'Why are you not dancing with the ship's officers this last evening at sea, like all the other girls?'

'Because no one asked me to, Mr. Lonza.' She smiled nervously as she answered him, for he was still a stranger to her.

'How formal you British are.' With lithe ease he swung off the steamer-chair and came to her side. He pitched the butt of his Russian cigarette into the sea, after killing it, and then before Lauri realized his intention he laid his hand over hers on the deck rail. 'What a cold hand,' he murmured. 'Are you nervous of me?'

'The sea breezes have chilled my hand,' she rejoined. 'I – I ought to be going down to my cabin – '

'You seemed content to remain here another hour, until you realized my presence a few feet away from you.' Amusement mingled with the foreign intonation of his words and made his voice extra fascinating, somehow. Lauri had not been alone with Michael Lonza before, and she was in awe of him as a *danseur noble*, and extremely aware that he was as dangerously attractive off-stage as on.

'Stay and talk to me,' he coaxed. 'I am rather lonely myself.'

'I can hardly believe that, Mr. Lonza.' Lauri looked at him with shy eyes in which a little laughter danced. 'I am sure every woman on board this ship would be thrilled to keep you company.'

'It is not the company of every woman on this ship that I want.' He lounged beside her and kept her hand a captive within his. 'I think you and I should get to know one another. We will be living at the same *palazzo*, sleeping under the same roof, and dancing on the same stage.'

'I shall be at the back of the stage, a very minor member of the *corps de ballet*,' she reminded him.

'What of that?' Laughter crinkled the corners of his eyes and intensified their charm. 'Our Director has not ruled a demarcation line between his chorus and his stars, which we must toe – besides, my Romany instincts tell me that you will not be for long a wood-nymph or a swan-maid.'

She tautened at his side as she felt him turn her hand palm upwards in his. 'The moon crosses your palm with silver and invites me to read it,' he said. 'I am half Romany, you know, and we have mysterious powers.'

'How fascinating,' she smiled. 'I suppose reading a palm by moonlight adds a certain magic?'

'Of course,' he agreed. 'The moon has always held sway over the hearts of women.'

'And the earth over men,' she capped him.

He chuckled, then bent his attractive gaze upon her palm, and though she believed he played a game, her heart beat fast as she watched him. 'Mmmm, I see two people in this small hand, a man and a girl destined to become friends – or lovers.' His fingers tightened about hers. 'I see also that you are not a person to seek the limelight. You shy from it – as from a flame – yet you are drawn inescapably into its white heat and the roar of applause that sweeps up out of the darkness like the sound of fire –'

'Please – stop!' Her hand struggled in his. 'You know I have reason to hate the very mention of fire –'

'What are you saying?' His puzzled eyes searched hers. 'I know only your name, and that you have never danced professionally.'

'But –' her eyes were raised wonderingly to his – 'it's uncanny that you should know how I feel.'

'I am sorry I touched on something so painful to you, Nijinka.'

She felt his sincerity, and told him quietly about her parents. 'I wish I could be anything but a dancer,' she sighed. 'But I suppose Signor di Corte is right, we must follow our destiny, our star.'

Her gaze was caught by a star overhead, which gave the curious impression of being pierced on that sickle moon, and Lauri gave a shiver. 'Several times you've called me Nijinka,' she said. 'What does the name mean?'

'It is Russian for tender one,' he replied. 'I think the name suits you. You are a tender lamb for di Corte to have brought into his company of swans and panthers.'

'Lonza the panther,' she murmured. 'People who dance in ballet always seem to get associated with graceful cats and birds, but I hope I'm not going to get tagged as Lauri the lamb.'

He gave a soft laugh, his head thrown back so that the blade of the moon seemed to shimmer across his throat. 'I will tell you something,' he said. 'When I saw you for the first time at that Strand Palace party, looking drowsy from several hours of ballet and one glass of champagne, I thought di Corte must be crazy to have signed up such a child. I am rapidly changing my mind about you. You are the sort a man has to discover slowly, and I am growing eager to see you dance.'

He gazed down at her, plundering the gold that glimmered behind her dark lashes, raking the soft scarlet of her unpainted mouth. 'I hope you are not one of those who has merely learned the mechanics of the dance,' he said. 'One can always hear that sort counting each beat of the music, concentrating earnestly like busy housewives watching eggs boil in a saucepan. Did you dance much at home?'

She smiled. 'In the summer I used to go up on the Downs near where we lived and dance under the sky in my bare feet.'

'Like Isadora Duncan,' he smiled. 'She brought freedom of movement into ballet, but she was not constituted to accept its disciplines . . . only to be a martyr to love. Have you read her life story, Lauri?'

He used her name like an old friend and she felt suddenly warmed. 'I try to read about all the famous dancers,' she said. 'Pavlova, Nijinsky, and the Signor's grandmother, Travilla. Do you mind having your dancing compared to Nijinsky's, Mr. Lonza?'

'You must call me Michael, little one. Quite frankly, I hate to be compared to anyone else. When I dance I am Lonza and no other man. It is true that I have Tartar ancestry, but unlike the great Nijinsky I don't cry in my soul for a lost and wounded youth. I enjoyed my youth.' He gave a chuckle. 'I was a dancer and a drifter; a wood-cutter and a peddler. Homeless as the Wandering Jew, and often as ragged as Lazarus. Then one day Maxim di Corte found me, as he found you, and I left the gipsy troupe with whom I was travelling and trained seriously for ballet.

'Our Director is clever and shrewd, Nijinka, but he is not an easy man to know. I believe he rather frightens you, eh?'

'I do find him rather alarming,' she admitted. 'He's so imperious and knowledgeable, and he expects so much. Does he ever take any of the classes at the *palazzo*?'

'Frequently.' Michael Lonza was looking rakishly sympathetic. 'He is a great teacher, and he will make you hate him before he makes a real dancer of you. He has a certain ambition, you know, which Lydia Andreya has never fulfilled – he wishes to give to the world another dancer like Travilla.'

'But Andreya is so exotic, so spellbinding.' Lauri gave him a look of amazement.

'Yes, Andreya knows how to bewitch an audience,' he agreed. 'She is a sorceress of the dance, and now and then, as at Covent Garden, superlative. But she lacks the fey innocence for which Travilla was loved, even after her marriage to Falcone di Corte. You see, people go to ballet to recapture the romance about which they dreamed before everyday life caught up with them, and now and again a dancer emerges who can give them romance. She is Cinderella, and Psyche. A breath of innocent wildness and joy, captivating as a bluebird, or a pixie spinner of moonbeams. Such a dancer never seems quite of this mundane earth. Andreya, who has been through the mill of a broken marriage, conveys bitterness and passion rather than romance.'

All that he said was true. Andreya had a striking face, Lauri admitted to herself, but to watch her dance was to have the feeling that she was poised on the brink of some inner torment or fury, to which she would have to give way. This created excitement and tension, but left an audience keyed up rather than enchanted.

Lauri recalled her own restlessness in Andreya's company at the Strand Palace party, her relief when Maxim di Corte at last put her into a taxi and sent her home to her aunt.

Her hands clenched over the deck rail as she stood in the moonlight, watching the white wake of the ship that carried her away from what she loved into the unknown. Towards Venice, where Travilla had lived with her husband after a stage accident put an end to her dancing career.

She had been born in Rome into a very poor family. Her mother was a laundress for theatrical people, and Travilla, then a child of eight, used to carry the washed and ironed linen to the actors and dancers at their lodgings. One of the dancers, Emilio Vanci, noticed her wild-bird grace and decided to become her ballet teacher.

She was trained and taught by Vanci until she was ready for her debut. Emilio was years older; a brilliant teacher and technician, but addicted to wine. He loved Travilla! It was always a well-known fact, but she danced into the heart of the distinguished Falcone di Corte, and went on dancing until the first night of *The Maid of the Moon*, a ballet created by Vanci, in which she sustained her injury ... her foot being caught in the 'moving mountain', a piece of spectacular scenery controlled off-stage by a lever. The ballet was withdrawn, and no other dancer had ever appeared in it. It was said to be unlucky, for Travilla never danced again, and Vanci died not long afterwards from a fall down the long flight of stairs up which Travilla used to run in all her elfin grace, a homemade dress fluttering about the slim legs that were to carry her across all the famous stages of the world.

Lauri drew a deep sigh, and then caught Lonza's thoughtful gaze upon her. 'Will you have a little supper with me before you go to your cabin?' he asked.

'But it must be very late,' she said hesitantly.

'What of that?' His teeth flashed in a smile. 'She who hesitates has no fun, and I know a steward who will bring us a midnight picnic up here on deck. Now stay here until I return – promise?'

'I promise.' She watched him stride away in search of the obliging steward, and it gave her the oddest feeling to remember the times she had studied Michael Lonza's photographs on the wall of her bedroom at Downhollow. The lean, daredevil face, and the mane of dark hair above the Tartar eyes. Only minutes ago those same eyes had smiled into hers, and the god of the dance had become a human being to her.

He returned carrying a tray on which stood a plate

of sandwiches, a bottle of wine, and a pair of stemmed glasses. He arranged their picnic on the foot of a steamer-chair and pulled another over towards it. 'Make yourself comfortable,' he said to Lauri, who still felt rather shy of him. She sat down and watched him pour the wine.

'May your future with the di Corte Company be long and successful.' He clinked his glass against hers, and captivated by his charm, she relaxed and lifted her wine glass to her lips. The wine ran warm through her veins, and as she bit into a sandwich she caught the sparkle of Lonza's eyes in the shadows.

'You are not at all the prim schoolgirl I expected when I learned that we were to be joined by a pupil of a ballet school,' he said. 'I made sure you would giggle and have pimples. I did not dream that you would have a husky little laugh, and eyes almost the gold of saffron – the colour of magic and romance, like the wine we are drinking.'

'What wine are we drinking?' she asked, her breath taken away by him.

'It is a Tokay, made to be enjoyed under the stars by a man and a girl. Do you find it heady?'

'Yes,' she gasped, tingling from the wine and the danger of being alone like this with a 'god of the dance' who was alternately gay and brooding. What would Maxim di Corte say if he could see them? Would he order her to her cabin, and remind her that dancers needed their rest if they were to give of their best? He demanded the very best. The heart and soul out of a dancer . . . not for himself but for the art he served, and the ambition that drove him in search of a dancer to follow in Travilla's magical footsteps.

Lauri finished her glass of wine and her sandwich, and

then rose to her feet. 'I must go to my cabin now,' she said. 'Otherwise when the ship docks tomorrow I shall still be asleep in my berth.'

Michael rose too. 'I should like to see you to your cabin –'

'No,' she shook her head quickly, for if other people saw them together it would somehow spoil the magic of their moonlit hour up here above the sea and the distant sound of music. 'Thank you very much for the talk and the picnic, Mr. Lonza.'

'Does it make you shy to call me Michael?' He took a step that brought him near to her. 'The picnics and the conversations need not end with the end of the voyage – I, for one, would like them to continue. Would you like that also, Lauri the lamb?'

She smiled uncertainly, for he had barely looked at her during most of the voyage and she couldn't help thinking that right now he was under the influence of the moon and the wine, and that in the morning he would lose interest in the reserved little English girl who was to dance in the *corps de ballet*.

'We'll see,' she said, and was about to draw away from him when the sound of footsteps on the deck planking froze her into immobility. It could have been the steward returning for their tray, but instinct warned Lauri that these footsteps belonged to someone taller and far less amiable than that little steward.

She turned her head and saw Maxim di Corte loom out of the shadows into the moonlight. His face was a chilly mask as he stood looking at Lauri, her dark head level with Michael Lonza's shoulder. His voice was even and quiet, but there was an undertone of anger in it as he reminded her that it was past midnight and time she was in bed.

His glance flicked the wine bottle and the glasses on the tray she had shared with Michael. 'I don't approve of my young dancers attending clandestine wine parties late at night,' he said curtly. 'And you, Lonza, should know better than to invite a mere child to one. I am aware that you are relaxing after a strenuous tour, but please remember in future that Miss Garner is not long out of the schoolroom, and that I expect her to commence learning our repertoire as soon as we are settled in at the *palazzo*. You yourself will be working with Bruno on the new ballet – there may, perhaps, be a part in it for Miss Garner.'

'Ah,' Michael drew in his breath, 'I thought you had something up your Venetian sleeve from the moment I really got to know this young lady.'

'Did you?' Maxim di Corte looked enigmatic as he shot out a hand and grasped Lauri by the elbow. 'To bed with you, *signorina*. Your eyes are swallowing your face.'

He marched her away from Michael, who called out gaily : 'Goodnight, Lauri the lamb.'

She felt Maxim di Corte looking at her, and her smile was sheepish as they walked side by side down the flights of stairs to the cabin she shared with two of his *corps de ballet*. In the dimly lit passageway, before he released her from his daunting presence, he said to her : 'Do you think of me as a taskmaster with a whip?'

There was an ironical smile in his eyes as he gazed down at her, one hand resting in his pocket, the half-light outlining the proud contours of his head and his well-carried shoulders.

'You don't need a whip,' she said, brushing a strand of dark hair back from her temple and revealing the tiny, velvety mole that clung to her white skin. Somehow it emphasized her fey look, her high cheekbones tapering to a soft, wide mouth; the gleam of gold through her black lashes.

'I am strict with my dancers for their own good, not to satisfy what you obviously think of as a dictatorial streak,' he said crisply. 'Ballet needs a rapier foot, flexibility, and senses always on the alert, and late nights blunt all three in anyone who is not a Tartar.'

'We were talking and the time just seemed to slip away,' she said in quick defence of the past hour with Michael. 'I was feeling homesick and lonely, and I'm grateful to Mr. Lonza for making me feel less of a stranger.'

The Director's eyes narrowed and glittered. 'The girls with whom you are sharing this cabin are very friendly. I told them to help you feel at home.'

'Please,' a look of alarm on their behalf sprang into her eyes, 'you mustn't blame Concha and Viola for my homesickness. They are pretty and popular, and relaxing also from a strenuous tour.'

'You mean they prefer the company of the young men on the ship,' he said dryly. 'Ah well, I suppose it is human nature for women to seek comfort from men rather than from their own sex.'

'Men do the same thing,' Lauri rejoined. 'I mean, they go to women to have their aches and pains soothed away.'

'I am not denying it.' He smiled in his enigmatic fashion. 'Not one of us is as self-sufficient as he likes to think. Always there comes a time when we have to admit that Nature has the upper hand and we are at the mercy of her whims.'

Lauri couldn't imagine this proud, haughty man at the mercy of anyone ... unless he referred to the tie which bound Lydia Andreya to a man who refused to release her so she could marry again. Anyone who loved was no longer self-sufficient, and he was always with Andreya. Walking beside her, listening to her, wrapping her in her sable coat when they went out on the deck to stand gazing at the sea; a striking couple whose eyes reflected a shared conflict.

'At the *palazzo* you will often find me strict,' Maxim di Corte suddenly warned Lauri. 'You have a lot to learn and I mean to teach you – even if you grow to resent me in the process.'

She caught her breath, for Michael Lonza had said the same thing and it alarmed her more than ever . . . made her even more aware of the gulf which separated her from home and the shield of Aunt Pat's love. She drew back against the cabin door and her fingers sought the handle.

'You child!' His eyes flashed over her face, with its winged eyebrows expressive of her desire to take wing from him. 'I shan't beat you if you put a foot wrong now and again, and the *palazzo* dungeons were long ago sealed up.'

'You won't be very patient with me,' she said, flushing under the mocking light in his eyes. 'Can you blame a mere member of the *corps de ballet* for being nervous?'

'Are you really more nervous of me than the young panther you have been so blithely alone with up on the promenade deck?' He took hold of her chin and made her look at him. His left eyebrow arched sardonically. 'Am I so very different from other men?'

'I think you are more demanding,' she said bravely.

'It would not do for the Director of a ballet company to be otherwise,' he said dryly. 'He controls a band of wayward and charming children; unbelievably talented and unpredictable. Think of the chaos that would reign if a director was too easy and indulgent. Petrushka would no longer act the fool, the Cruel Doll might weep, and Albrecht refuse to carry his bunch of arum lilies.'

Lauri had to laugh, and at once she felt the seal of his ring pressing into her chin. She was held like a bird in the hand, and as she met the compelling eyes of the man who had taken control of her future, she felt her heart beat fast with a fear which held a strange fascination.

'Talent, like a gem, lies buried in clay which must be chipped away piece by painful piece,' he said. 'The process cannot be avoided, Miss Garner.'

'What will happen if you keep on chipping away at me only to find clay?' she asked.

'I shall be very disappointed in my own judgment,' he replied quizzically. 'In a private conversation which I had with your aunt, she agreed with me that in Venice you might be able to lay aside your fears and forget your ghosts. I hope so. Venice is rich in history, a city that should appeal to you very much. Let its magic enter your heart, *signorina*.'

He then let her go, leaving the pressure of his seal upon her white skin. '*Buona notte*,' he said, and strode off before she could wish him goodnight.

She gazed after his tall figure until he disappeared into the gloom at the end of the passageway, then she entered the cabin and was relieved to find her two companions curled up asleep in their berths. She undressed and slipped noiselessly into bed, where she lay for a long time lapped by the rhythm of the ship.

When she finally fell asleep she dreamed of a palace like a fortress, with a tall tower built against one wall. In a room at the top of the tower dwelt a man who wore a mask. He frightened her, yet she felt compelled to mount the spiral staircase that led to him. She wanted to tear off his mask, but at each step she took he drew farther away from her, and she felt she would never get close enough to find out what he was like behind his mask.

CHAPTER FOUR

THEY disembarked at the port of Zattere, and the journey across the lagoon to the *palazzo* was made in a launch. They heard the noon bells pealing as they passed the great Campanile of St. Mark's, where rows of black gondolas were tied up like the canoes of warriors who had gone ashore to take booty and captives.

Lauri smiled at her own flight of fancy, and turned to gaze back at the Doge's Palace, like something out of a fairytale, and the huge golden domes of the Cathedral above which a thousand pigeons fluttered until the bells grew quiet again.

Spring would come to Venice any day now, but this was the time of the year when this city of fretted steeples, arcaded buildings and old palaces was safe from the invasion of the many tourists who would arrive in the summer with their cameras and their guide-books. This was Venice at its best, its sunshine filtered by a breeze that kept the canals fresh and sparkling.

They passed a barge laden with boxes of market produce, and turned into a waterway where sunlight and shadow flitted over scrolled balconies, climbing plants and painted shutters. Water swirled across the steps of arched doorways, and there was an atmosphere of bygone days, and signs of Venetian script on the weathered walls. A gondola swooped by and Lauri glimpsed the strong dark face and almost balletic grace of the gondolier.

Excitement caught at her heart . . . this was a city to fall in love with. Already it was casting a spell over her.

She turned from gazing after the gondolier to find the dark eyes of Maxim di Corte fixed upon her. For several seconds she couldn't withdraw her gaze from his, which was as direct as that of a Titian. The entire look and manner of the man blended in with the medieval aspect of the city to which he belonged. In him there was an element of shadow, but something about his mouth and his eyes gave warning of hidden fire.

'Venice is fascinating, *signor*,' she felt compelled to say, aware of Andreya's strange eyes through cigarette smoke, unsmiling and intent.

'Not by daylight.' Andreya flicked ash at the peeling plaster of an old house that might once have been a patrician dwelling.

'Like a once beautiful woman, Venice needs the cloak of dusk and the soft sparkle of stars to make her glamorous once more,' Michael Lonza remarked, a faint smile narrowing his eyes and a hint of hidden meaning in his words. Andreya's cigarette hissed in the water, and with relief Lauri felt the speed of the launch slowing down. They were heading towards a private landing-stage set in front of a great stone house whose upper half overhung the water in the form of a *piazza* guarded by an ornamental balustrade.

At the side of the house there was a single tall tower, which held Lauri's startled gaze as the launch drew in against the water-worn steps that led up to the landing-stage, where a gnarled old man waited with a boathook. He held the launch steady as one by one they mounted the steps and gathered in a group in front of the *palazzo*, its walls mellowed by centuries of sun and water-sparkle to a tawny grey.

Lauri's gaze was fixed on the tower about which she had dreamed so strangely last night on the ship. She could, of course, have seen a picture of it in the book of memoirs by Travilla di Corte, but all the same it was mystifying that in every detail her dream tower resembled the reality. Instinct also told her that there was a spiral staircase inside, winding up to the rooms behind those narrow windows, under the roof set round with battlements.

She didn't have to wonder who lived in the rooms of that old and romantic tower. Who else but the master of the *palazzo*!

She glanced at his tall figure in a stone-grey suit and saw that he was studying his impressive old home with the intentness which he gave to everything . . . almost as though he wished that Travilla could appear again on the *piazza*, a winsome figure in white, leaning over the coping to greet him with a loving smile.

His group of dancers grew restive and began to chatter in various languages, and the men set to unloading the piles of baggage from the launch. Michael Lonza left his companions to get on with the unloading. He strolled with lithe grace to the entrance of the *palazzo* and stood gazing at the enormous wooden door in which a grille was set at eye level. Dominating the arched portico was a fierce stone falcon holding lightning in its claws.

'Falconry – sport of the knights.' Michael turned and leaned against the door. 'I think you still fly them, *maestro*. Slim, jewel-eyed creatures who flash upon their prey without warning and take their hearts. Is it not true, *signor*, that in the old days the falconers punished severely any man who dared to fondle their dark-plumaged pets?'

'A female – and most falcons used for hunting were female – should have only one master. Come, Miss Garner, let me welcome you to the Palazzo Falcone.'

Lean fingers barely touched her elbow, and yet in the grip of compulsion she walked with Maxim over his threshold into the great chilly hall with its marbled floor. Venetian mirrors and lanterns gleamed duskily, throne-like chairs stood about, and dark panelling lined the walls. The hall would have been forbidding but for a ceiling that glowed with scenes from medieval Venice, a pageant, a feast for the eyes painted by a Venetian master who had lived in the days of carnival and intrigue, elopement by gondola, and family feuds that led to duels.

Long, long ago this old baronial hall had echoed to the laughter of those Titian ladies and their gallants, as they watched the antics of the Punchinellos. Harlequin in his motley might well have slipped a note into a small, white hand, while a cloaked boatman waited to row the lady to her lover.

A great horseshoe of a stairway led to the upper rooms, and the peace that had reigned over the *palazzo* for several months was broken as the rest of the company flocked in, demanding to know where they were to sleep, and when they were to eat.

'Lorenzo . . . Giovanni . . . !' The master raised his voice and the servants came running. Miraculously, within less than an hour the dancers were unpacking in their rooms, while down in the great cavern of a kitchen a beaming Venetian woman who liked noise and the laughter of young people bustled about preparing coffee and food for them.

To Lauri's relief she was given a small room of her own. She was a girl who rather enjoyed solitude, and after she had unpacked her case and hung her few dresses in the old-fashioned wardrobe, she opened wide the batwing shutters at the window and thought how strange it was to be living in a palace on the water.

The water swirled below, jade and sapphire, and Lauri felt as though she had arrived in a city of fantasy. She reached eagerly for her writing-pad and pen, and sat down by the window to write Aunt Pat a letter describing the *palazzo*. Words like rambling and romantic leapt to her pen, and her nostrils quivered as she described the smell that hung in the air, that of water-lapped stone walls and hoarded sunshine. The gilt was tarnished on the great mirrors and portraits, she wrote, the Florentine brocades that swagged windows and alcoves were worn and faded, but there was still something rather sumptuous about the Palace of the Falcon.

Her pen suddenly faltered and her eyes grew wet. Aunt Pat must be feeling very lonely at Downhollow all on her own. If only it had been possible for her to come to Venice, but the atmosphere was too damp for someone who suffered from arthritis. 'All I ask,' she had said to Lauri, 'is to see you dance in ballet as I never could, up near the footlights, the star of the show.'

Lauri gazed out across the waters of Venice, and her tears dried on her lashes. When you loved certain people you wanted to please them, to live up to their expectations of you, but it was very difficult at times. Especially when your heart held other, elusive longings.

She sealed her letter and addressed the envelope, and went along to the room Concha and Viola were sharing to ask them how she went about posting a letter. Several of the dancers spoke English, Concha among them, and she told Lauri to put her letter in the basket she would find on a table down in the hall.

'I'd rather like to go out and post it myself,' Lauri said, for she was eager to explore the neighbourhood and had noticed there was a bridge at the side of the *palazzo* which gave on to a *calle*. A *calle*, according to her guide-book, was a street or an alleyway.

She mentioned the bridge, and Concha said at once that the *calle* on the other side led to a small shopping square, where she would find the local post-office in the grocery store. 'Are you sure you will be all right?' Concha added, sweeping rather anxious eyes over the slight English girl in a tweed skirt and a tomato-coloured jersey. 'Dusk falls quickly in Venice, and it is all too easy for a stranger to get lost.'

'I'm a country girl with a good sense of locality,' Lauri smiled, waving her letter as she ran off down the grand staircase. Her purse was in the pocket of her skirt, and her jersey was a warm, hand-knitted one. She caught a glimpse of herself in one of the huge mirrors as she crossed the hall – an elfin creature with a dark switch of hair hanging down over one shoulder.

The *palazzo* was fronted by a fairly wide pavement that led round to the side of the building, where a small stone bridge arched across the canal to a cobbled street. Lauri sped light of foot across the bridge and upon reaching the other side she glanced back at the rambling *palazzo* with its single tall tower. One of the two hundred palaces of Venice, where she would be staying for several weeks. It was a disturbing thought, and yet as Aunt Pat had said, not every girl had the chance to live for a while in a palace . . . very much at the command of its Venetian overlord, Lauri added to herself.

She hastened on her way to the post-office, which she duly found in a quaint grocery store. The woman behind the counter was accustomed to dealing with tourists and she was able to understand that Lauri wished to buy stamps for her letter. This bit of business concluded,

Lauri turned to a display of fruit and bought herself a bag of little plums that were like drops of gold.

Having escaped from the *palazzo*, Lauri was in no great hurry to return. She wandered along by a canal eating her plums and tossing the stones in the water, breaking for a moment the reflections of the houses with washing hung from old iron balconies. Now and then a gondola sped by like a black swan, its gondolier a lean, weathered sculpture as he handled the great oar with grace and skill. She noticed that the gondolas held boxes and packages of goods . . . not the romantic couples of fiction, gazing dreamily at one another as their gondolier sang an opera ballad that echoed over the water.

Lauri was vaguely aware of having lost all sense of time, but it wasn't until she found herself in an old courtyard, beside a stone well-head surrounded by gar-goyles, that she realized how the afternoon light had deepened. Pink flames quivered in the sky, and a sudden breeze plucked at her hair. Gosh, she had better be getting back to the *palazzo* before it grew any darker!

She turned to make her way out of the courtyard and saw old houses looming up all around her. There were twin archways, left and right, which led out to canals at either side of the courtyard, and even as she took a few steps to the right, she glanced hesitantly over her shoulder at the glimmer of water beyond the other archway. She could, in her abstraction, have wandered in through either one of them, and was quite at a loss to remember which one it had been.

For a moment she felt utterly stranded in this old city square with a well in the centre. She couldn't speak a word of Italian, so it was no use knocking on one of those high wooden doors. Neither was it any use getting into a panic. She listened, and when she heard water splash softly in the gathering dusk, she ran out under the nearest archway and saw a slim craft gliding towards her.

'*Pope*,' she called out, a word culled from her guide-book which meant that she wished to hire a boat. This one swooped in against the stone quay and the dark eyes of the gondolier flicked her slim, lost-looking figure.

'Palazzo Falcone – *please*?' she entreated.

He nodded and helped her into the gondola, and as a melancholy beauty settled down over the canal, Lauri was rowed home to the *palazzo* sitting amidst sacks of vegetables and several crates of melons.

She hoped she would not be seen when she alighted at the landing-stage, but as she turned from paying for her ride, she blundered into someone tall who caught at her with hands that were none too gentle. 'Where have you been? You have had us concerned for you.' She was swung round, and with a gasp found herself face to face in the light of a wall-lamp with the very person she had hoped to avoid . . . the *padrone* himself.

'I had to post a letter, and I wanted to see something of Venice.' She was on the defensive because in a way she was at fault in having wandered beyond the limits of the post-office. 'Don't tell me we have to give notice of our intentions before we're allowed out of the *palazzo*?' she said flippantly.

'Don't be a child.' A thread of steel gave his words a cutting edge. 'You went out without a cup of coffee or anything to eat, and I am responsible for your welfare, let me remind you. If you wished to explore a little, then you could have asked someone to go with you who is used to the intricacy of our waterways. Water has an alluring quality, Miss Garner. You follow it and before you know where you are, you are lost. This happened, of course.'

It infuriated her that he was so certain, and so right. 'A moment ago you told me not to be a child,' she said. 'It's because I don't wish to be dependent on other people that I went out on my own. One learns through one's blunderings, *signor*. As a director of ballet dancers you should know that better than anyone.'

'Yes, perhaps I was mistaken to call you a child,' he allowed, a quirk to his firm lips. 'You have a woman's ability for turning a man's argument against him, because few women like to admit their mistakes.'

'Why do men always have to generalize about women?' The gold flashed in her eyes. 'It's human nature to be self-determined, so why should men possess the royalty rights to independence and expect only humble submission from women? If a man chooses to do something, then it's always right, no matter how crazy. He can tear himself to bits in a fast car for the sake of a speed record, and he's a hero. Or fall from a mountain of ice out in the middle of nowhere, leaving a widow and several children, and he's called a sportsman. Men are the babies, if you ask me!'

'You evidently feel very strongly about the rights of women.' There was amusement in the deep voice above Lauri's head, and with a sense of surprise she found that he had guided her through a side door into the walled garden of the *palazzo*. An illuminated fountain gave out a green light that turned shrubs to goblin shapes, and tall cypresses into giants.

There was a scent of myrtle, a rustle of ilex trees, and the dimly-seen tassels of flowers. The fountain itself was shaped like a great stone goblet, and the tinkling of water was echoed by the twitter of a night bird.

Lauri didn't wish to linger here with Maxim di Corte, but she had to because she wasn't sure of the way indoors.

'How did you enjoy your first ride in a gondola?' he asked.

'It was loaded with vegetables, so it wasn't exactly a romantic ride.' She drew back against a tree, and finding it a willow she put up a hand to finger its veil of leaves. Willow trees made her think of Downhollow and the little cottage where she had always felt so secure. Now she was out in the world, alone among strangers like this tall rather forbidding Venetian whom no one had ever humbled or hustled in his life.

Her fingers clenched on the willow leaves, for there was no denying the vibrancy about him which seemed to quicken one's awareness of everything. Suddenly she was very aware of being alone with him in his Venetian garden, with the moonlight silvering the tips of the cypress trees. She glanced away from him up at the moon, a shyness clutching her by the throat.

He followed her glance. 'The half moon upon which Pierrot rides through the sky,' he murmured. 'To drift in a gondola is like riding on the moon, do you not think so?'

'As I said, my one was half loaded with vegetables.' She tried to speak lightly, but her voice shook a little with an emotion that felt a little like fear. It quickened her heart, and made her bones feel strangely weak, and as though he sensed this he drew nearer to her and she saw the smile that gleamed in his eyes.

'You must find yourself a companion among the other dancers to go exploring with,' he said. 'I insist on this.'

'You are fond of insisting,' her fingers crushed the

willow leaves, 'but I happen to enjoy my own company, *signor*.'

'Do I understand from this, *signorina*, that you have never enjoyed the company of a boy, and the pangs of calf-love?'

She knew that he was teasing her, but all the same she blushed and felt very immature. Most girls of near-eighteen had been out with boys and been kissed. She could not imagine what a kiss was like . . . and her eyes widened as the moonlight cast a shadow over the autocratic face of her Director, leaving only his well-moulded lips and jawline below the mask. The lower lip of that firm mouth was fuller than the thinly-cut upper lip, hinting at Latin passions held in rein but there all the same.

'Innocence is an intriguing quality, Miss Garner,' he said. 'There are male dancers in my company who will quickly realize that there is about you this unique quality.'

'I can take care of myself.' The colour deepened in her cheeks at being taken for a prize ninny who didn't know the first thing about men. 'If you are referring to Mr. Lonza, then I can assure you that his interest in me is purely professional, *signor*. He told me last night that he was curious about my dancing ability.'

'Surely he also told your fortune?' There was a sardonic note in Maxim di Corte's deep voice. 'I believe it is one of his favourite gambits, and irresistible to the feminine temperament. What did he tell you? That a tall, dark man lurks in your path and that you must beware of him?'

He laughed, moon-masked as he raised a hand and released her fingers from the willow leaves they were crushing. 'Tomorrow you begin work under my tuition,

Miss Garner, and we will not get along very well if you are going to be as tense as this all the time.'

'Your tuition, *signor*?' She looked alarmed.

'Yes, mine.' He quirked a black eyebrow. 'Any objections?'

She shook her head, dumbly, and hoped that tomorrow would never come, or that he might take pity on her and hand her over to that gentle teddy-bear, Bruno, his *régisseur*. 'Come,' he led the way indoors, turning upon her that searching gaze of his as they entered the hall where the Venetian lamps were now alight. The panelling gleamed like the light on dark armour, and the shabby grandeur of the Venetian furniture was gilded by the golden lamps.

'A little alarm is justified,' he said dryly, 'but don't overdo it. Your private life is your own, so long as it does not interfere with your dancing, but I should not like to see your fledgling wings scorched and that is why I offer you a warning about Lonza. By all means let him amuse you, but guard your heart for greater things.'

'For ballet, do you mean?' She was amazed at her temerity in speaking up like this to a man who could intimidate with a mere glance. 'I realize very well, *signor*, that you demand of a dancer that she give heart and soul to the art of ballet – but I don't know whether I can promise to do that.'

'Indeed?' He frowned down at her, and she felt her bones grow weak again. When he frowned like that he seemed capable of anything – of sending her supperless to bed, for instance. An absurd thought, which made her smile faintly even as her gaze was caught and held by his dark one.

'It is my opinion that you don't know for sure what you do want,' he said, a trifle grimly. 'But you will grow up one day, and then you will discover that much of what we do in this life is not entirely in our own hands. We all fight against this, of course, but fate has its will of us.'

'Even of you?' she exclaimed. Even of this man of iron and black velvet, whose mastery over the will of others was something to marvel at.

'Even I, *signorina*.' His smile began in his eyes, a star-flash that made her draw back from his tall figure until she was brought up short by the baluster of the great staircase.

'What a fatalist you are,' she said shakily.

'*Che sara sara*.' He shrugged his shoulders. 'It is bred into Latin bones, this awareness that destiny is not to be escaped – but right now I will let you escape to your room. Dinner is at eight-thirty. We dine late in Venice, as in all Latin countries where the evenings have a magic of their very own.'

He gave her a formal bow, then turned and strode into a room with double doors made for the entrance of a giant. Lauri ran all the way up the great staircase to her room, which was tucked away in the corner of the gallery. She hastened inside, closed the door behind her and leaned her back against it. Her heart beat faster than she had ever known it to beat. Her cheeks were hot, her hands cold as she pressed them to that fiery warmth.

Whatever was the matter with her? She had not felt so alarmingly *aware* and yet fragile since that bout of 'flu she had had two years ago. She drew a long, shaky breath. It was Maxim di Corte who had made her feel like this, with his face out of the Roman past, and his way of talking . . . as though destiny was something that stalked you, silently, until it pounced.

She switched on the light and gazed around the room in which she would be sleeping for the next few months. The massive 17th-century bed seemed to fill up most of it, with its carved posts almost reaching to the ceiling. The curtains that had once draped it had been removed, and it had the look of a monarch stripped of all glory but for a counterpane on which was embroidered a medieval lady in still gorgeous colours.

Hours of patient needlework by one of the ladies of long ago who had lived here; a bride of a Falcone di Corte perhaps.

Finding a jug of hot water on the wash-stand, Lauri stripped off her jumper and skirt and began to wash. There was a bathroom a few doors away, but she had heard someone splashing in the tub as she had run by a few minutes ago. The best time to take a bath, she conjectured, was early in the morning when her companions on this gallery were still fast asleep.

Having dried herself and used her talcum powder with a lavish hand, she went to the big carved wardrobe and inspected her small stock of dresses. She didn't know whether she was expected to dress formally and decided to compromise by wearing her wine velvet skirt and the white lace blouse which Aunt Pat had knitted her.

She braided her dark hair and arranged it around the crown of her head. This evening she felt an inclination to look a little older and more sophisticated.

She studied her reflection in the Venetian mirror, and wondered if it was the scrolling around the frame that made her look curiously medieval. Her cheekbones seemed higher, her eyes more tilting, and her lips fuller. Her neck, she decided, looked as vulnerable as a swan's, and she was about to let down her braid when a brisk tap on her door interrupted her.

Leaving her hair as it was, she went to the door and opened it. 'Hullo!' The gay, brown eyes of Michael Lonza swept her from head to toe. 'Mmm, you look different. Not at all like the schoolgirl who stirred the bubbles in her champagne with the tip of her finger.'

'When my hair is up like this I – I feel like Swanilda,' she laughed, confused by his admiration and not at all sure that it was justified.

'It makes you look a young lady of dignity.' He smiled and bowed and offered his arm. 'May I escort you down to dinner, madame?'

They walked towards the stairs, her fingers looking pale against the dark material of his dinner-jacket. The company's first evening at the *palazzo* after a tour was always a form of celebration, he told her. They also dressed formally when important patrons of ballet came to dine, but apart from that they were more or less free of Maxim's guardianship when their practice or rehearsal day was over. Quite a few of them, he added, went out to the Café Anzolo for ravioli.

'I would have taken you out this afternoon, Lauri, if you had intimated that you wished to see something of Venice.'

'I had a letter to post to my aunt,' she explained.

'I heard that you got lost.' He slanted her an oblique grin. 'Gossip of any sort travels like wildfire among a group of dancers, and from her window one of the girls saw you alighting from a gondola – straight into the hands of our Director. She said you looked ruffled, and he rather grim.'

'He's very bossy,' Lauri said, a flush in her cheeks. 'He thinks I'm a child and incapable of taking care of myself, and I've been ordered to get myself a friend to go exploring with.'

'To ensure that you don't go astray, eh?' Michael's eyes were agleam with devilry as they met hers. 'It will be a pleasure obeying his order, don't you agree?'

She looked puzzled, and he added teasingly : 'I told you on the ship that we were going to be friends – have you forgotten so soon?'

'You meant what you said? It wasn't just the wine talking, Mr. Lonza?'

He seemed to find this remark highly amusing, and as he started to laugh, Lauri found herself joining in. Their laughter mingled as they reached the foot of the stairs . . . just as the master of the *palazzo* came striding through a door set in a shadowy part of the hall. He paused, and stood gazing with intentness at the laughing couple who were as vivid against a background of dark panelling and marble columns as a pair of Tiepolo lovers.

There was a golden quality about Lauri's eyes in laughter, but this quickly gave way to confusion as she caught sight of Maxim di Corte. In evening clothes he was even more overwhelming, his Roman distinction and air of cool command being thrown into prominence rather than tempered down by the sober black and white. Also he was gazing at her and her companion with his eyes fairly glittering under the black arches of his brows.

'It is to be hoped,' he said as he came forward, 'that you dance as well together as you look. Tomorrow we will see !'

It was an order, and Lauri glanced in alarm at Michael as their taskmaster strode ahead of them into a large *salone* where most of the other dancers were already assembled for aperitifs. 'Don't look like that,' Michael gave her hand an encouraging squeeze. 'There is nothing to be nervous about in dancing with me. We are in accord, you and I, and we will dance like angels together.'

She smiled nervously and had no doubt that he could dance like an angel with the clumsiest of creatures. 'But, Michael,' his first name slipped out, 'I couldn't possibly dance with you in front of all the others. I – I should die!'

'I wonder.' They stood there in the hall of golden lamps and shabby grandeur, the young male dancer leaning down to the slim figure in wine velvet and a shell of lace as though about to lift her in a *pas de deux*. 'Have you ever read how the divine Isadora Duncan danced impromptu with Nijinsky in a Venetian palace? They knew nothing of each other's style, but when they rose to dance it was as one person because of their inborn knowledge of the dance, and the *rapport* that can exist between two people, sometimes for only an hour, sometimes for a lifetime. For Isadora and Nijinsky an hour was enough.'

'I am only Lauri Garner, not one of the Divines,' she said simply.

When they all sat down to dine, Lauri became separated from Michael at the long, feudal table, islanded with heavy silver, and flowers and wine in crystal containers. The dancers at either side of her couldn't speak much English, and she sat silent, without much appetite, very aware of Maxim di Corte at the head of the table, with Andreya beside him dispensing wit with all the pointed charm of a woman of the world. Her hair was swirled to the crown of her head and secured by a calot of jade. Her medieval styled dress was sashed by more jade, the strange colour of her eyes.

'Miss Garner,' all at once Andreya's voice floated down the table on a lull in the general conversation, 'I hear that tomorrow you are to show your paces as a dancer – but why wait until tomorrow? We would all enjoy seeing you dance tonight.'

Lauri felt her heart turn over as she met Andreya's brilliant, mocking glance. And then Maxim di Corte said crisply : 'There is no need to look on the verge of flight, Miss Garner. You will not be expected to dance before an audience just yet.'

'Why not, Max?' Andreya lifted her wine glass and took a demure sip. 'What is there for her to be nervous about? We will make allowances for her amateur mistakes.'

'Get on with your dinner, Lydia.' He was frowning.

His frown, however, held less power to quell when it came to his *prima ballerina*. 'Are you afraid we will laugh at you, Miss Garner?' she enquired silkily.

Everyone at the table was looking at the two, and even those who spoke no English were aware that Andreya was challenging the new girl, the shy little thing with gold in her eyes – and perhaps gold in her feet.

She felt small waves of sympathy coming from some of them, and knew that timidity would never be admired by a company such as this one. 'Have you no other jester to entertain you at the banquet, Madame Andreya?' The words leapt from Lauri's lips, amazing even herself, and causing a suppressed giggle from Concha, who was craning round the muscular frame of the character dancer who sat immediately beside Lauri.

Andreya raised an eyebrow at this flash of spirit from Lauri. 'I am merely inviting you to dance for us, little English Miss,' she drawled. 'Take a look around the table. See how eager everyone is to see what you can do – or not do.'

There was drama in the air and everyone was sensing

it. Maxim di Corte's frown had deepened, and Lauri knew that in a moment he would change the conversation in his decisive way. A demon of defiance seized hold of her. She would show him, as well as Andreya, that she was not a child who had to have a shepherd, and whose decisions had to be made for her.

'Yes, I'll dance tonight,' she said clearly, 'if Mr. Lonza is willing to be my partner?'

A gasp of excitement ran round the table. Michael was leaning back in his chair, his eyes agleam in his lean, swarthy face. 'Of course I am willing.' He raised his wine glass to Lauri, openly saluting her courage in not backing down to Andreya. 'My Romany instincts must have warned me that tonight we would dance, Nijinka, for I have eaten as sparingly as a monk.'

There was a burst of laughter. Lonza a monk! The eyes of the girls sparkled with amusement as they looked at the lean, agile Tartar whose creed was that the brief feast of youth should not be wasted.

All at once Maxim di Corte was on his feet, a commanding figure who silenced the sudden outbreak of excited comment with a sweep of his hand. 'Very well,' his gaze settled darkly on Lauri's pale young face, 'if you wish to dance for us, Miss Garner, then indeed you shall dance. But let me warn you that you will have a very discriminating audience. Like the truffles most of us have been enjoying,' he shot a sardonic glance at Michael, 'dancers are born of thunder and have lightning in their veins.'

'Their directors also, Max.' Andreya gave a laugh that held a rather off-pitch note. 'Did not a thunderstorm shake Venice the night you were born? Travilla writes an account of it in her memoirs.'

At mention of Travilla, his eyes blazed darkly,

engulfing Lauri for a moment, then with a flick of his table napkin he sat down. 'Let us proceed with dinner,' he said. 'All of us, that is, who will not be dancing a *pas de deux*.'

Lauri hardly knew how she got through the next half hour. She was conscious all the time of curious and eager eyes upon her, and it was with relief that she left the room at the end of the meal to go and change into a ballet tunic and dancing slippers.

Her demon of defiance had wilted a little by the time she had changed in her room and gone through her warming-up exercises. Oh heavens! She drew a deep, shaky breath. Suppose she made a fool of herself in front of Maxim di Corte!

CHAPTER FIVE

LAURI came alone down the grand staircase of the *palazzo*, a slim figure in a simple tunic, walking in her ballet slippers as though on sword points.

Her nervousness grew when she saw the entire company assembled in the hall, some of them seated on chairs and sofas, others sprawled on the floor in the graceful attitudes which dancers can achieve so readily. A fire of logs burned in the cavernous fireplace, and the gold velvet curtains were closed across the long windows. Maxim di Corte was supervising the laying of a felt mat across the floor, directly beneath an ancient tapestry that would serve as a backcloth for the *pas de deux*.

Andreya sat enthroned in a carved Italian chair, her long fingers drumming the ornate arms. Bruno Lanning stood beside her, but when he noticed Lauri at the foot of the stairs he came strolling across to her. Bruno was partly American, a brilliant ballet-master whose hair was always on end from a habit he had of thrusting his fingers through the grey thatch. He was a retiring sort of person, who was at his best, Lauri had heard, when he was teaching the dancers a new ballet or putting them through the paces of a traditional one.

'All set to slay di Corte's lions?' He stood ruffling his wiry hair as he smiled down in his kindly fashion at Lauri.

'All set to be slain, Mr. Lanning.' Her hand clenched on the baluster of the stairs as she saw Andreya looking across at her with a cold intentness. She shivered and felt like a martyr about to enter an arena of lions. 'I don't know what I was thinking of to let Andreya needle me into this,' she added despairingly. 'I – I can tell from the Signor's manner that he's angry with me – '

'When the Director looks fierce like that,' Bruno cast a glance over his shoulder and smiled, 'it sometimes means that he is pleased.'

'Pleased?' she echoed, her bewildered eyes on the tall, dark-browed figure as he wheeled a lovely old harp to the edge of the felt matting. She watched as his long fingers strayed over the mother-of-pearl inlay, surely the gesture of a man who loved beauty and would not hurt sensitive things?

Her own hand gripped the carved baluster as he came striding across the hall towards where she stood with his *régisseur*. He might have stepped down from one of the portraits that hung upon the panelled walls; all that was missing was the doublet and hose, and a long, crimson-lined cloak.

'Your orchestra awaits you, Bruno,' he smiled. Then his eagle eye was sweeping Lauri from head to toe, taking in her wand of a figure in the ballet tunic. Before she could move his hand was covering hers on the baluster. '*Cielo*, you are cold as a little frog!' he exclaimed. 'Come over to the fire while we wait for Lonza – or would you like to call off the performance?'

'And disappoint everyone, *signor*?' She felt his touch, so vital and warm, so seemingly concerned, and the next instant had snatched her hand from beneath his. 'I want to dance – with Lonza.'

'I want you to come and get warm,' he insisted.

She shook her head, for Andreya was sitting over there with the other dancers grouped nearby.

'She has temperament, you see, Bruno.' An amused gleam came into Maxim's eyes as he studied her. 'There is a ballet called *Lurline and the Knight*. Do you know it, Miss Garner?'

She nodded. *Lurline* was one of the first ballets she had learned, and a favourite of hers because of its enchanting story.

'Do you think you could dance the *pas de deux* with Lonza?'

The suggestion took her breath away, and he immediately accepted her breathless silence as acquiescence. 'Good.' He thrust his left hand into his dinner-jacket pocket and withdrew something that gleamed golden. 'Here is the magic talisman for you to give to your Knight,' he slipped over her head a slender chain on which hung a carved topaz heart . . . the heart which Lurline gives to her Knight to protect him in battle, though she dies herself in parting with it.

Lauri fingered the gem, which hung against her fast-beating heart, and instinct told her that the topaz was real and not just an imitation. Would it be a magic talisman and help her through the ordeal that, in all fairness, she had wished upon herself?

She glanced up at Maxim, her eyes reflecting the deep-gold of the heart. 'It's valuable,' she said hesitantly. 'Are you sure – ?'

'Yes.' His nod was almost curt. 'Ah, here comes Lonza!'

'Good luck, Lauri.' Bruno gave her an encouraging smile as he went and seated himself at the lovely old harp, and a ripple of excitement ran through the hall as Lonza came running down the stairs, lean and lithe in a silver-mesh doublet and black tights, transformed into a being out of a world Lauri had never seriously thought to enter . . . the magical world of ballet.

'Have you told Lauri that you wish us to dance the

pas de deux from *Lurline?*' Michael gave her a brief wink as he spoke to their Director.

'Yes.' Maxim captured her eyes and held them with his. His gaze was magnetic, his voice low and deep as he said to her : 'Forget your audience, forget everything but your interpretation of Lurline. She is a girl so deeply in love with a man that she is prepared to die for him. She is a forest being who knows he will fall in battle unless he is protected by her heart, which has been turned to stone but is softened by love. If you make the role real enough, exciting and magical enough, then you need not fear your audience – or anyone. Do you hear me?'

She nodded, feeling herself mesmerized by him.

'You are a girl *infelice in amore* – remember.' His brilliant smile flashed over his face, then he was striding across the hall, and gesturing at Bruno to begin the music.

Lonza took Lauri's hand and led her on to the felt matting. 'Oh, Michael,' she whispered, 'I'm terrified. I – I can't remember a step of the ballet –'

'Don't try,' he whispered back. 'We are not about to dance in a theatre, and what you forget I can always cover up with a little improvisation.'

His hand squeezed hers, and a little consoled, she gazed around and saw the expectant faces softly shadowed by the Venetian lamps, and the great tapestry behind her and Michael, glowing with a forest scene. She felt a compulsion to glance at Andreya, but fought it, knowing it would unnerve her to meet the ballerina's unsmiling and critical eyes. She looked instead at her partner, and gave a tiny gasp as in obedience to the music he swept her into the first movements of the *pas de deux*.

In those first moments Michael did everything he could to cover up Lauri's nervousness, a strong partner, superbly at ease in handling her and guiding her. It was when he projected her into the first off-balance position of the dance that she came fully awake to the fact that she must do her part and not leave everything to him. The harp music rippled through the hall like Pan-pipes, and suddenly like a being enchanted Lauri was dancing without timidity, feeling Michael's breath fan her forehead in a soft laugh as he arched her over his thigh.

She lifted a hand to his face as he drew her up the length of his lean body to his shoulder, leaping with her, pagan and exultant. She stretched her pointed feet in the air until they were talons, flicked them, and came down softly, silently, spinning round in Lonza's arms and breaking from him to stab the stage in a rapid run.

Her dancing now was truly that of a creature of the woods, and she flashed around her partner until suddenly made captive again and carried aloft on his shoulders. When he swept her through the air, she took wing and he seemed to hold her back from flying away. And because she wore a tunic and not a *tutu* he was able to come in close to her and almost brush her mouth with his . . . a dark and dangerous lover, with a jag of black hair clinging to his forehead.

From far away Lauri seemed to hear quickened breathing as she and her partner went through the feints and attacks of their love-dance. There were ripples of laughter as she played the rogue and eluded his arms. A taut silence as the moment came for her to stretch on full *pointe* and slip over his head the talisman that would always protect him, though she could not live now she gave him her heart.

She drew away from him, assuming a poignant stillness. Her hair had become loosened – the long hair once the symbol of enslavement, something for the invader to catch hold of when a woman attempted to run away. Lonza leapt and as though trying to hold her back from what was taking her, his fingers twined in her hair until she came close to him, held captive for the last time. In her stillness she had to express the double fear of dying and wanting to remain with him. She pressed closer to him, but even as triumph lit his eyes, she slid down his body and out of his grasp, flying to the ends of his fingers.

All was still, and then she sank to her knees, abandoned like a little animal to the pain, the dread and the final loss. Lonza knelt, he stroked the dark wing of hair over her face, cradled her, rocked her as they exchanged a kiss of death.

There were no curtains to close and cover them, so Lauri could not struggle free as Lonza's kiss deepened, his lips holding hers as a wave of applause broke over them. 'You sweet thing,' he breathed. 'I don't think you have ever been kissed before.'

She flushed, broke free of him, and was aware of running past Maxim di Corte as she made for the stairs, for the sanctuary of her room and refuge from the reality that had broken so shatteringly into her dream world.

Her lips still felt the pressure of Michael's, and she carried with her into her room the dark blaze of Maxim di Corte's eyes. Whenever he looked fierce, Bruno had said, it meant he was pleased! She hoped she had pleased him tonight, for after those first faltering moments she had danced as never before in her life.

Tiredly she stripped off her practice clothes and slipped into a robe. Moonlight filtered into her room when she opened the curtains, and she stepped out on to her small balcony and stood listening to the rippling of water against the stone walls of the *palazzo*.

Venice . . . a city drowned in legends and lagoons, only the lap of the moonlit water to be heard in the night.

A silence that all at once was broken by the sound of voices rising from the *piazza* just beneath Lauri's balcony. She was about to retreat into her room when her name was mentioned, and all too human, she had to stand and hear what was being said about her. 'Do you think I don't know why you brought that Garner girl to Venice?' There was a note of hysteria in the woman's voice. 'You mean to partner her with Lonza in the new production of *Giselle* – you think she will dance the role better than I because she is younger –'

'Lydia, must we indulge in this quite unnecessary scene?' Maxim di Corte's voice held a note of strained patience. 'I have made no explicit plans regarding the girl, and that is the truth.'

'Don't deny that like the rest of the company you noticed how well she looked with Lonza. You noticed all right! Young, so dewy fresh that I would like to kill her – *ah*, my wrist, Max! You – you are hurting me!'

'How often must I tell you that you don't have to be jealous of anyone?' he grated. 'You are Andreya . . . beautiful and bewitching, with a following no young dancer could hope to achieve for a long time.'

'You hurt my wrist,' she said petulantly. 'You are ruthless, Max, and if you thought to replace me in *Giselle* you would do so.'

'You hate the role, it always upset you, but I would hardly let a mere child dance it in preference to you, Lydia,' he rejoined. 'The girl shows promise – she would not be with us otherwise – but others in the company have more technique, more experience –'

'Others in the company have not that certain look, Max –'

'What do you mean?' He sounded very angry now, and Lauri on the balcony above flinched for Andreya.

'You know well enough what I mean.' Andreya spoke defiantly. 'I have studied your own special portrait of Travilla often enough to recognize that this girl has the same look of elfin innocence, as though she dwelt always in the woods among the fairy folk and had no idea what real life was all about.'

There was a startled sort of silence, during which Lauri could have counted the beats of her heart. A breeze stirred through her dark hair, and she could feel her own tenseness as she waited for Maxim's reply.

'There is a physical resemblance,' his voice carried clearly to Lauri's ear, 'but that cannot make up for what is otherwise lacking.'

'This English girl lacks something important, Max?' Andreya's voice had grown honeyed, as though at last he was saying something to her liking. Lauri's hands clenched the coping of her balcony, and it hurt more than she liked to admit to hear Maxim di Corte say that she lacked something when tonight she had thought she had pleased him.

'It grows late, *coccinella*,' she heard him say to Andreya. 'I think we will go in.'

'You have not called me *coccinella* in a long time. I love you too.' A note of intimacy came into Andreya's voice. 'It reminds me of that first ballet in which I danced for you – Max, do I still dance as I danced in *The Ladybird*? Be honest with me.'

'I am always honest with you, my dear,' he replied.

'You always dance with seduction and witchery. You are Andreya – is anything else important?'

'You are, Max. I – I would be lost without you, *caro*.'

'Nonsense', he said, and then a silence fell and Lauri sensed that the ballerina had been drawn into the circle of Maxim's arm. Though a man of depth and discernment, he was obviously bewitched by Andreya's beauty, indulgent of her jealousies towards his younger dancers. Lauri felt suddenly cold and she withdrew into her room and quietly edged her balcony doors together. She took up her hairbrush and automatically brushed her hair, counting the strokes as though they helped to counteract her thoughts.

All was quiet, except for the rippling of water against stone, when she slipped into bed. Tonight she slept in a palace. Cinderella who had danced and been kissed. . . .

A kiss could be comforting and exciting, she supposed, but in front of Maxim di Corte it had been rather humiliating. Her cheeks burned against the coolness of her pillow. Did he think her brazen because she had submitted to Michael's kiss in front of him, and the rest of the company? But she had been taken by surprise, and was too helplessly shy of men to know how to handle their inclinations, and their oddly uncomfortable moods.

She sighed, and wondered again what it was she lacked in Maxim's dark, eagle eyes. Whatever it was, he needn't have told Andreya just to make her purr.

In the following days Lauri was put through her paces in a practice room that was sparsely furnished with some chairs, a huge wall mirror, and a *barre*. These lessons with Maxim di Corte lasted two hours, and at the end of them she joined the rest of the dancers. They had coffee and rolls, then rehearsed with Bruno the ballets that were lined up for the new season. The ballroom of the palazzo made a vast and impressive practice room for them.

They were a close-knit group who spent a great deal of time together. They discussed ballet in each other's rooms, where they also mended their tights, darned ballet slippers, quarrelled in a good-natured way and made up again.

But it wasn't all work. They all loved Venice, and boat outings were frequently enjoyed. In the evenings groups of them went out to dine at a local café, where Venetian music was played, and where the atmosphere was always gay and informal.

It soon became apparent to Lauri that her fellow dancers regarded her as Michael Lonza's 'little friend'. Several girls far prettier than herself were openly envious, others were amused. Watch out, they warned her, the Panther is a dangerous charmer and very fickle.

Lauri had guessed this long ago, but she wanted to see all she could of Venice and he seemed to enjoy showing her around.

Sometimes when they were alone in a fascinating old courtway, or drifting along in a gondola, a wicked little glint came into his eyes and she would guess the trend of his thoughts. 'If all you want is a lot of foolish kissing, Michael, then you had better not take me out,' she said to him one afternoon. 'Kissing is for people in love, and I don't care if you think me old-fashioned and square for saying it.'

'How will you know you are in love, or not, if you refuse to let a man kiss you?' he teased.

'I'm not falling for that one, clever Mike,' she rejoined. 'Falling in love is a serious matter, and I don't intend to think about it until I'm at least twenty-one. I may never think about it, in fact.'

'You will eat your words before we leave Venice, Miss Prim,' he warned. 'Don't you know that two people who dance perfectly together are bound to fall in love?'

'I don't dance perfectly according to Signor di Corte.' She gave a wry little laugh. 'I am informed that if I wasted five minutes on-stage as I did at the start of our *Lurline pas,* he would fire me from the Company.'

'I doubt it, my pet.' Michael lounged against a statue in an arcade of St. Mark's Square, where they sheltered from a spring shower. 'Next time you are alone with the Maestro, take a good look at that stubborn chin of his. The man thrives on challenge, and you, being a female, challenge him even more than I did when I agreed to give up my vagabond ways so he could make a real dancer out of me. If you knew what I was like then, Nijinka!'

'I imagine you kicked up the dust wherever you went,' she laughed. 'Did the Maestro have a hard job taming you – as far as you can be tamed?'

'We often came close to a fight,' Michael admitted. 'He then taught me to fence and whenever our tempers flared, we fought it out with Italian foils. Now and again it is still necessary for us to cross swords, but he did what he set out to do, he made a *danseur noble* out of a Romany wanderer who thought of dancing as an easy way to earn money for a glass of wine, or a meal.'

'It's strange,' Lauri murmured, 'how you have to bow down to the man even though he makes you hate him. No matter how well you think you've done a *fouetté* or a *pirouette,* he always finds it less than perfect, and though you want to aim something at him, when you do the *fouetté* as he suggests, you see at once that he's right. He's infuriating, and tireless. Sometimes I crawl out of that practice room, but does he care? No! "Have a cup of coffee," he growls. "You are young. You will soon survive my treatment and revive." '

Michael laughed out loud, and a raindrop fell from the jag of hair that lay across his forehead. His laughter echoed across the empty square, where pigeons huddled under stone eaves, and the pavement of the Campanile shone wet. The Laguna beyond was hazy, a little melancholy.

'I find you very refreshing, Lauri.' He gave her dark braid a light tug. 'You are a deep one, but now and again you bubble in a most unexpected way. You "walk between passion and poetry", as Wilde once said. You are a little out of reach, and that beguiles me. You see, I don't take you on these Venetian tours because I hope to be rewarded in the usual way. I like just to be with you, to watch your eyes light up the dimness of an old church, to see you stroke all the brindled cats and avoid like a superstitious little witch the black ones.'

'I like all cats,' she protested. 'I just don't like a black one to run across my path.'

'*Scaramanzia*, touch wood,' he mocked, his eyes glimmering in the deepening shadows. 'You women are all beautifully mad. Look around you at this moment – is this Piazza in the rain-wet dusk not a setting for romance, or tragedy? Othello could come stalking out from one of those archways . . . or armoured knights climb down from their base.'

It was true, Lauri thought with a little shiver. The atmosphere was rather supernatural as the day waned, bringing with it the violet hour. The rain had left pools in which the pigeons bathed, and there was hardly a soul about. Lamps began to glimmer along the water-edge of the Campanile, and there was a rustle like silk as the evening breezes stirred the Laguna.

'We ought to be making our way home,' she said.

'I thought we might have dinner together at the Café of the Three Fountains,' he suggested. 'You have never been there, Lauri. It is quiet, the food is good, and we can eat in peace without having to listen to a lot of talk about ballet.'

'But you love ballet, like all the others,' she exclaimed.

'I enjoy risotto, but I can't eat it all the time,' he rejoined. 'I like the music of Ravel, the books of Thomas Mann, and arguments about technique with Maxim – but not all the time. Tonight I want to dine at the Three Fountains, to watch the stars in the water, and be a man with a girl. Don't you want that as well?'

Yes, she realized. She wanted to forget all about ballet for a few hours . . . to be free of the man who was her master each morning at the *palazzo*. Controlling her every movement, her every inclination, as though she were a marionette with no human feelings. 'You are not tired,' he would say. 'Come, we will go over that *pas de bourrée* again, and this time you will use your legs with grace, not as though they are sticks of celery!'

Sometimes it seemed to her that he had a heart of stone. It didn't matter to him that some days she ached with homesickness; that Andreya could make her feel very much the British interloper – all he cared about was the dance.

'Your body is like a violin to a musician,' he would say. 'Care for it, watch your Achilles tendon, never wear worn-out slippers, and always have a rub down after you have finished exercising or practising.

'Ballet must be lit by a magic combination of style, wit and magic,' he emphasized, 'otherwise it is a static one-dimensional picture instead of a three-dimensional one.'

His authority as a teacher was absolute, and to rebel against his commands was to find herself being put firmly in her place. All the same, her technique was improving, and she grudgingly admitted that what he didn't know about ballet would have fitted beneath the ruby of the poison-ring which Andreya wore.

They all knew it was a poison-ring. Viola had once seen it lying on the ballerina's dressing-table and she had taken a good look at it. The tiny aperture under the ruby was empty now, but long ago – in the days of the Borgias – it had needed only a slight movement of the hand to tip the lethal contents into somebody's glass of wine.

Lauri was wondering how a woman could bear to wear such a ring, when at her side Michael raised his voice in order to hail a passing gondola. 'Come along,' he caught at her arm and they ran across the Piazzo to where the swan-prowed boat awaited them.

'We're not really dressed for a smart restaurant,' she said, as Michael assisted her into the craft. She was wearing a jacket over a skirt, with a wine velvet cap perched on one side of her head. He was just as casually clad.

'This is Venice, where people dress to suit themselves, not the conventions.' Michael sat back in his one-armed seat with its fringed black cushions, and the warning cry of their gondolier echoed across the water as they swooped beneath a bridge and around a narrow corner.

As they drew away from the Byzantine domes of St. Mark's into the deep, mysterious waterways, their gondolier seemed to get the idea that they were sweethearts and he decided to serenade them. His voice was un-

trained but strong, and Lauri listened fascinated as his
Venetian song resounded against the walls of the old
palazzos, the cloistered warehouses and workshops whose
projecting windows almost touched overhead.

The gondolier smiled down at Lauri as he sang with
gusto the old song of Venice that tells a girl to marry
young, to marry while the leaf is green because youth
is soon lost.

The song died away and all that was left was the
ripple of water beneath the gondolier's great paddle.
But he had made magic for Lauri and her eyes shone
softly as she gazed around her, smelling the old drowned
walls and watching goblins of light dance on the water.
She had never dreamed in England that Venice would
be so strangely enchanting, so captivating in all its
moods.

No wonder Maxim di Corte brought his dancers here
to recuperate, and rehearse for their next season. Though
she didn't begin to understand the man, she realized that
as Director of his team he was beyond reproach. He
knew the needs and feelings of dancers as if they were
his own; that they were beings as full of emotion and
imagery as the lovely ballets they brought to life on-
stage.

Venice was ideal for them. *'Ma Venezia ze la sola.
Che me posa contentar.'* The bells across the water
making music as they exercised and mimed, and learned
carefully their roles in the forthcoming season of ballets.

'You are very quiet.' Michael's voice roused her from
her reverie and she gave him a smile. He should be
wearing dark hose, she thought. A velvet jerkin with
slashed sleeves, and a plumed *berretta*.

An answering smile kindled in his eyes. 'You are glad
you agreed to come with me to the Three Fountains?'

'Did I agree?' Her mood had grown quietly gay. 'It seemed to me, you Tartar, that you abducted me.'

'What a Tartar likes, *dushamoya*, he takes.' He took her hand, and as she glanced up and saw their gondolier sculptured tall and dark above them, her heart missed a beat. For a strange moment it was as though Maxim di Corte stood there . . . reminding her of something she had forgotten completely until this instant.

'Michael,' she gasped, 'there are to be important guests at the *palazzo* tonight. We are all expected to attend for dinner.'

'I had not forgotten,' he drawled, 'but I always find those dressy affairs so boring. Don't you?'

'That isn't the point.' Her hand struggled in his like a captive bird. 'Signor di Corte will be annoyed with us – the other dancers are bound to put in an appearance – '

'If the others attend, then he may not notice that we are absent.' Michael squeezed her hand. 'Relax, Lauri. He will be too busy with his guests to give us a second thought. It is just that there are feudal strains in the man and he likes to show off his vassals to the well-to-do people who invest money in the company.'

'You mean he thinks it a good business policy to let possible investors see what they are getting for their money?' Lauri frowned.

'You have it in a nutshell, my pet.' Michael lowered one eyelid in a wicked little wink. 'Maxim di Corte's dancers are the flames that entice the moths. We are no more than that at these dinner parties at the *palazzo*.'

'Then I'm glad this one slipped my mind.' Lauri was no longer worried about being absent from the dinner party, which was being given for the Contessa Riffini and several of her friends. The very thought of titles and tiaras made her feel nervous.

'Look, we approach the *isola* on which the Café of the Three Fountains is situated.' Michael pointed out the lights twinkling among the trees of the small island, and Lauri heard music drifting across the water. A few minutes later their gondola drew in against a stone jetty, and Michael paid their boatman and went ahead of Lauri to give her a hand up the water-worn steps.

'Dinner on a little island is much more to my liking,' she smiled. 'You do have charming ideas, Michael.'

'I am gratified to hear that I can charm even you, you cool British Miss.' He escorted her from the jetty towards the sound of music and the glimmer of lanterns in the dining-garden of the Three Fountains. Tables were set under the trees, and a smiling waiter led them to a table near a fountain of nymphs and fauns, with a gush of white flowers arising from the basin in place of water.

The air was drenched with the fragrance of syringa and plum-blossom, while on their table gillyflowers were arranged in a bowl, shy and pretty things, velvety under her touch.

'This garden is idyllic,' she said to Michael. 'Just smell that syringa.'

'First I wish to smell some good food. Now what shall we have to eat?' He consulted the menu with enthusiasm. 'Mmm, how about some Adriatic fish with a half-bottle of Falerno to start us off? Macaroni with the fish, I think – they cook it with tomatoes, butter and a little onion. It's delicious.'

It was indeed delicious, and evasive on her fork. Michael showed her how to attack the creamy strips, to subdue and sustain a buttery forkful. Their wine, he said, was the same the Romans of ancient times enjoyed.

They lingered over their meal in this garden on an island, listening to the musicians who wandered from table to table; watching the gondolas glide by like black swans.

Avanti was a word they had never heard, and they gaily clinked their glasses together and laughed to think of their fellow dancers on their best behaviour for the Contessa. 'I hate starched shirts and manners to match,' Michael said as their peach dessert flamed in the waiter's ladle and the toasted almonds crackled. 'Give me freedom. Give me laughter and love. Do you not agree, *dushamoya,* that they are the most important things in life?'

She thought that finding love was very important, but she wasn't sure that her companion's regard for love was quite the same as her own. 'Peach with almond is heavenly,' she said. 'The taste is somehow pagan.'

'I am glad to hear that you have a taste for the pagan,' he said wickedly. 'I discover you slowly, Lauri, peeling the petals, as it were, from off a thistle.'

'What a romantic description,' she laughed. 'Am I so prickly?'

'As a little hedgehog at times.' His smile was speculative. 'Would you like me to speak romantically to you?'

'No indeed. Please get on with your peaches and almonds.'

'Come, are you afraid you will like it?' He studied her face in the lantern light, delicately hollowed and touchingly young. Her lips were darkly red, slightly moist from the wine they were drinking – wine of dreams, of youth, of sadness.

'Do you think I don't know that you fight your own dreams, your own longings in order to please your aunt . . . and the *grande signor,* who sees you as another Travilla?'

'Please, Michael.' She went cold, as though touched by a ghost, and the enchantment began to die out of this supper *à deux*. 'I'm not another Travilla. I haven't her ability – or anything else.'

'You have not seen Maxim's portrait of her, up in that Venetian tower of his.' Michael leant towards her. 'In some lights, with your dark head a little inclined and your lashes making shadows on your cheeks, you might have sat for that portrait. I saw it the night we talked together on the ship. He must have seen it at once – and how that calculating heart of his must have leapt to the fact that you were also a dancer.'

'Stop it!' She jumped to her feet. 'I want to go home!'

'Home?' Michael's eyes narrowed. 'Do you mean to England?'

She stared at him, and felt a sudden wild and impossible longing for England, for her aunt, and the quiet cottage life they had led. 'No, silly,' she forced a smile to her lips. 'Home to the *palazzo*.'

It was late when they arrived back at the *palazzo*. The Signor's dinner-party was long over and most of the lights were out . . . all but one that glowed behind a narrow window high up in the tower where he had his apartment.

Built long ago, that tower, solid and tall in the starlight. Michael saw Lauri looking up at it, and he gave a rather mocking laugh. 'What is the matter?' he asked. 'Were you afraid he would be waiting up to scold the pair of us?'

'Of course not,' she said, though something of the sort had entered her mind.

'Come, you know you are afraid of him.'

'I am nothing of the sort.' She hurried ahead of Michael into the *palazzo*, and hated to admit to herself that she looked forward with apprehension to her lesson next day with her dark master.

CHAPTER SIX

LAURI was apprehensive about her lesson with Maxim di Corte the following morning, but it turned out that she didn't have to face him for a few more hours. Bruno informed her at breakfast that Maxim would be away for a day at least, attending to business connected with the Contessa Riffini. Lauri breathed a sigh of relief. He might not remember when he returned that she had been absent from the dinner party he had laid on for the Contessa.

She attended Bruno's class and after a strenuous two-hour practice, he bade his pupils take chairs and proceeded to talk about the great exponents of dancing and how they had achieved their perfection.

They had stamped their personality on a particular style of dancing, he said. There had never been a Sylphide quite like Taglioni, or a Dying Swan like Pavlova. Never a Spectre of the Rose like Nijinsky.

Bruno wandered about the room, hands clasped behind him, a look of rapt pleasure on his face as he talked about the gods and goddesses of the dance. 'We come to Travilla,' he announced. ' "A swallow in flight . . . a sport of Psyche." She was nothing less, my children. She became part of the music and danced upon it as on a beam of light. When you watched her you realized that each dance step is truly a variation on the heartbeat. Unlike some of the other great *prima ballerinas* she danced not for the world – as was generally supposed and accepted – but for one man, her husband. But in dancing for him, she answered an eternal plea in all men, touched a universal chord in all women.'

'Were you acquainted with her?' one of the dancers wished to know.

'In the last years of her life, long after she was compelled to retire from ballet,' Bruno replied. 'But I saw her dance often when I was a youth. My father was a government official and my parents lived in various cities all over the globe. Often we were fortunate enough to be in the cities where Travilla was appearing.'

Cups of steaming coffee were brought in at that point, along with seeded rolls thick with butter and smoked sausage. After the first pangs of youthful hunger had been satisfied, the talk reverted to Travilla.

'People say she was beautiful,' spoke up a young male dancer. 'In pictures I've seen of her she struck me as being rather plain.'

'Few pictures have done justice to her elusive attraction.' Bruno wiped his lips on a large bandanna which he used for mopping his neck and forehead when he was putting his class through their paces. 'On-stage she had a strange, fey beauty. In the changing, jewel-toned lighting she was a bird of paradise . . . a fluttering thing that every boy longs to catch. She made of the magical a reality for a few golden hours, so that we in the audience were drawn in, made a part of her world.'

Lauri listened to all this with fascination, for Bruno could speak half a dozen languages and he translated all that he said into English as well as French and Italian. Now he translated a question that made her go tense in her chair.

'Do I think there can ever be another Travilla?' He looked thoughtful, and perhaps it was only by chance that his glance rested for a moment on Lauri.

'I am a hopeful man, a believer in fairy tales, otherwise

I would not be in this mad and wonderful business called ballet.' Bruno smiled in his shy way and thrust his hands through his hair. 'And now, my children, the debate is over and we will proceed with some work.'

Lauri was one of a quartet dancing in The Magic Jade, a new idea of Bruno's about a jade figurine that comes to life at night in an auction room. A young man desires the figurine and he hides in the auction room in the hope of having the jade to himself for just one night.

It was exactly the sort of ballet to appeal to Lauri, and the remainder of the morning passed enjoyably for her. Lunch was served in the dining *salone*, and afterwards she attended the mime class until five o'clock. In ballet all movement must have a meaning, and the hands, the eyes, the entire body of a ballet dancer should speak silently and eloquently.

Michael Lonza sometimes attended the mime class, but not today, for he was working with Andreya on the new production of *Giselle*, in which he danced the princely role of Albrecht.

It was well known in the Company that Andreya disliked the role of Giselle, but she was the *prima ballerina*, and Concha confided to Lauri that she had been known to dance with a pulled ligament rather than let another dancer take her place, even for one performance. She clung to all the leading roles as firmly as a moray-eel to a rock, and anyone chosen to understudy her might as well sit in the wings with some knitting.

'I wonder why Andreya dislikes the role so much?' Lauri and Concha were enjoying ravioli at the Café Anzolo.

'Andreya is vain, like all great beauties, and she knows that she will never dance *Giselle* as it was danced by

Travilla. She is intensely jealous of the memory of Travilla,' Concha added gleefully.

At the end of the meal, Concha wanted to go with a group of dancers to a late art exhibition; Lauri felt disinclined for further company and made her way back to the *palazzo* alone. When she reached the forecourt she stood gazing up at the tower that looked as dark and impregnable as the man who had his apartment up there.

There were no lights behind the narrow windows of his rooms. His tall figure did not stand silhouetted against the stars, for tonight he was away from home and the tower had a strangely deserted look.

Lauri went a step closer to the rough stone walls and gazed with fascination at the door set deeply in the wall. It seemed to her to have an air of hiding the forbidden. It intensified her curiosity about Maxim di Corte's eyrie; the tower-study in which he kept his collection of books on the ballet . . . and his own special portrait of Travilla.

She put out a hand and tried the handle . . . to her half-frightened delight it turned and the unlocked door swung inwards with a ghostly little creak. A winding staircase confronted her, illumined by lamps set in wall niches spaced rather wide apart, making a spiral of up-winding, shadowy light.

Her heart beat fast . . . the temptation to mount those stairs was overwhelming. It would, she reasoned, take her about five minutes to reach the battlements. She would steal a quick look over the city from the roof of Maxim di Corte's tower, then scuttle down the stairs and be out of the door like a shadow that had never entered in the first place.

Shadows and slight rustlings followed her all the way to the top landing. There she paused and took note of

a trio of oval-shaped doors. Two of them gave access
to Maxim di Corte's private rooms, and suddenly she
felt a trespasser and wished she had not given in to the
impulse which had brought her this far.

A draught tickled her neck and she turned towards
the door behind her. Now or never, she thought, and
swiftly opened it. A sigh of relief escaped her as cool
night air came drifting down several stone steps. She
mounted them and found herself out on the battlements
of the tower.

She stood beside one of the deep embrasures, the wind
flattening her dress to her slim figure, awed by the dim
shapes of the towering steeples and immense domes that
seemed closer up here. The scene was Gothic . . . she
breathed the night and the mystery into her very being,
and felt under her fingers the lichen that covered these
old grey stones.

Overhead the stars were like small white flames, and
the scent of the waterways drifted upwards with each
distant ripple. From here, Lauri thought with a smile,
the fair Rapunzel could have let down her hair for her
sweetheart to climb. Here the brooding power of Maxim
di Corte had a setting both wonderful and lonely. An
eyrie fit for a lofty idealist, a man as unyielding as iron
when it came to art and its proper expression.

Was he different, a little more human when alone up
here in his tower? she wondered as she took a final look
at the great domes the Venetian voyagers of long ago
had erected as their monuments. The wind blew cool
through her hair, loose on the shoulders of her dress of
rowan-red velvet. It was her favourite dress and she
didn't really know why she had put it on to go to the
Café Anzolo. It was an informal place, and Michael
had not eaten there tonight.

Perhaps as Concha had suggested he had taken out another girl. Lauri knew she had annoyed him last night by hurrying him away from the Three Fountains just as he was enjoying himself.

Right now she must hurry away from this place. Each second that she lingered added to the danger of running into Maxim di Corte. She turned round . . . and the most uncanny feeling swept over her as she was about to cross the tower. She sensed rather than saw anything among the shadows. Heard an infinitesimal rustle that could easily have been the wind brushing against the lichened walls of the tower.

A cold shiver ran through her. She wanted to cross the battlements and make her escape down the spiral staircase, but was held back by an instinctive fear of the unknown . . . a remembered awareness of the soft rustlings which had followed her up the stairs. *The silk about a woman's ankles would make such a sound.*

As in a dream she stood fast; her limbs were leaden though her heart was racing. Were those whispers among the dancers true? Was the tower *haunted*?

Nonsense, she scoffed, though still she didn't move. All dancers had far too much imagination, and she must snap out of this and not imagine that something stood shadowy, waiting, on a bend of those winding stairs. . . .

A gasp of fright escaped her as footfalls rang distinctly on the stone steps leading to the battlements. A shadow loomed up, larger than the others, and again she took a step backwards.

'Be careful,' the voice was lash-sharp with warning, 'there is a crack in that wall!'

She was against the wall, the sound of water lapping ominously against stone far below her, when Maxim di Corte swept her close to him in a pair of arms that felt iron-hard. 'You little fool,' his breath raced across her forehead, 'you might have been killed!'

'I – I didn't know it was you.' She could feel his hands right through the velvet of her dress, bruising her until he let her go as suddenly as he had taken hold of her.

'Who else were you expecting?' His eyes narrowed as they raked her frightened face. 'This is my tower. I issue the invitations.'

'I – I had no right to come up here,' she stammered. 'You have every right to be angry with me.'

'I am angry because you could easily have had an accident, Miss Garner.' He drew her away from the embrasure that in daylight was like blackened teeth. 'Some years ago lightning struck this tower and weakened the structure, that is why I prefer you dancers to keep to your own section of the *palazzo*. Come, you can stop shaking in your shoes. It is a wise girl who never trespasses, but a feminine one can never resist temptation.'

'The view is wonderful.' She gave him a shaky smile. 'I've often seen you up here admiring the lovely old buildings and waterways.'

'I know which parts of the tower are safe,' he rejoined. 'If you wished to see the view from here, you should have asked me and I would have brought you up here one evening when the sun was setting over the city. Why did you never ask?'

'You're a busy man, *signor*,' she could feel herself flushing in the gloom. 'I didn't like to bother you – '

'It would not have been a bother,' he said crisply. 'I am always happy to talk about Venice. Do you find it a fascinating city, *signorina*? Has Michael Lonza shown you all the places you should see? The Byzantine churches, the galleries, the islands where they make lace, and Venetian glassware?'

'He has talked about taking me to Murano,' she could feel her flush deepening and turned slightly away from the dark eyes that might discern it. 'I love looking at anything made of lovely old glass.'

'The finest age of Venetian glassware was in the sixteenth century, and I have an ancient goblet from those days which you might find interesting. What of the museums, Miss Garner? Have you been to any of those?'

'One or two.' A smile quivered on her mouth. 'I'm afraid Michael finds them rather a bore, except for the sumptuous Venetian costumes and the ornaments and swords the people used to wear with them.'

'They are very striking, I agree. This section of the tower is quite safe, if you wish to go a little closer to that embrasure, Miss Garner. I shall not snatch you off your feet as before. Poor child,' his laugh was a little mocking, 'I don't quite know how you regard me – as some ferocious baron, perhaps? In which case it was either foolhardy or brave of you to venture up here – just for the view.'

'It was plain nosiness, *signor*, as you said yourself in a more subtle and Latin way.' She peered over the embrasure at the canal below, lap-lapping the stone quay of the *palazzo*. 'Are there mermaids in the canals of Venice, who dwell in the underwater palaces?' she murmured.

'It could well be.' There was a smile in his voice, and she felt the brush of his sleeve as he stood beside her. 'Venice is a mysterious city, almost a fable in itself, and when the steeples and domes meet their shadows in the water – as we are told they must in the end – then all things lovely will be gone.'

Lauri gave a little shiver and he must have felt it,

for he said crisply: 'Venetians have a melancholy strain in them, as well as subtlety. Tell me, Miss Garner, where did you go last night? I had promised the Contessa Riffini that I would introduce you to her. She was disappointed at not meeting my little English dancer.'

'I – I forgot all about the dinner party, *signor*. I'm sorry.' Lauri had to force herself to turn and face him; she felt sure his anger was awful when roused, and all day she had been fearing the moment when he would demand an explanation for her absence.

'Lonza was also absent.' His voice was silky, more coldly menacing than when he lost his patience in the practice-room. 'I can assume that you were together? That you found each other's company of far more interest than the company of my friends?'

'I didn't imagine for one moment that I would be missed.' Lauri stood braced against the lichened wall of the tower, slender in her red velvet, and afraid of his frown. The frown joined blackly above the bridge of his Roman nose . . . sign of a man who would not wed, said the country-folk of Downhollow.

'You are altogether too modest,' he mocked. 'Lonza would not wish for your company if you were a colourless nonentity, Miss Garner. Where is your Romeo tonight? Are you taking a rest from the excitement of his company, or did you plan to meet up here? I recall that my arrival on my own tower gave you a nasty surprise.'

'You exaggerate, *signor*.' She tried with a smile to win him back to his earlier mood. 'A trespasser expects to be surprised if like an idiot she lingers too long on someone's private property. I'm truly sorry about last night. I did forget, and then it was too late for us to get back for the party – '

'I accept part of your explanation,' he drawled. 'No doubt Lonza persuaded you to forgo the party altogether. Where did he take you?'

'We had supper at a restaurant on a little island. The Café of the Three Fountains.'

'I know the place. It is very romantic and secluded. And now perhaps, to make up for not being at my table last night, you will join me for supper in my tower? It is my servant's evening off, but he has prepared a cold-fowl salad for me, also there is fruit, and coffee.'

Even as Lauri was taking in the unexpectedness of the invitation, he was placing his hand beneath her elbow and leading her with decision towards the steps that descended to his rooms. A minute later she was being ushered into a lamplit room whose dark panelling was mellowed by framed drawings and pictures of ballet artists. There was also a packed gallery of books that encircled the room and was reached by a small winding staircase.

'Please to be seated, Miss Garner.' He indicated a tapestry sofa beside which a table was set with chessmen. 'Do you play?' he asked, as she leant forward to look at the ivory knights, castles and bishops with pointed hats.

'I'm afraid not.' She shot him a smile. 'A game of draughts is about all I can manage.'

'Chess is a fascinating game.' His eyes flicked her dress, and her dark hair that fell rain-straight almost to her slender waist. 'A game in which knights storm castles and challenge queens should have a lot of appeal for someone like you, *signorina*.'

'You make me sound very young,' she protested, 'as though I still believed in goblins and Galahads.'

'Don't you?' He quirked a dark eyebrow, then turned

aside from her and flicked a hidden switch. Immediately a portrait glowed into vivid life against the dark wall-panelling. A large portrait whose enamel-like tones depicted a girl dressed in an embroidered blouse, flounced skirt and lace-edged apron. Her dark hair was crowned by a headdress of tiny leaves and flowers.

The room was strangely silent, and then Maxim turned to look for a searching moment at Lauri. 'Travilla,' he murmured. 'As she appeared in her favourite role – Giselle.'

Lauri couldn't take her eyes from the portrait . . . it was as though she had always known the girl.

The artist had not flattered or detracted, he had portrayed with warmth the youthful grace of spirit and body which had been Travilla's. Her eyes were softly alight, her lips half-parted in a smile were sensitive yet gay; her neck was very slim and vulnerable to have been bowed so frequently under the mighty sword of acclaim . . . which can fall more swiftly on the great than on anyone else.

Unconsciously Lauri's hand was near her heart, as though to still its beating. 'Her eyes speak out of the portrait,' she whispered. 'One can almost hear the rustling of her dress . . . as though at any moment she will step down out of the frame and dance for us.'

'I always think of the portrait as enchanted,' he agreed, and feeling his gaze Lauri turned to look at him. She was shy of being alone with him in his tower; aware of a subtle charm in the atmosphere – an undercurrent of danger.

She felt him reading her thoughts, and lowered her gaze with the delicacy of a little cat. The undergold of her eyes gleamed through her dark lashes.

'When we have had supper,' he indicated a side-table

on which stood silver-domed dishes, a bottle of wine
cradled in a basket, and a bowl of fruit, 'I will show
you some small possessions of Travilla's which I think
you will find rather charming.'

'I shall look forward to that.' She smiled a little at
her own demure reply, her fingers finding the edge of
a book under a crimson cushion of the tapestried sofa.
When she knew that Maxim had gone to the side-table
and had his back to her as he carved chicken, she withdrew a slim volume and let it fall open where a silk
marker lay between pages of verse. They were by Yeats,
and one of them had been lightly underscored, as if of
special significance to the owner of the book.

Lauri scanned the lines, and they lingered in her mind
after she had returned the little book to its hiding place
behind the cushions.

> I have spread my dreams under your feet,
> Tread softly, because you tread on my dreams.

They charmed and intrigued Lauri, a slim young
figure in Dante-like velvet. Under whose feet had Maxim
spread his dreams – the swift, stabbing feet of Lydia
Andreya?

He made a domestic clatter at the table behind her, a
man whose power and passion were revealed by his approach to his work. He would love a woman with great
intensity, Lauri felt. He would be like Falcone di Corte
who had never looked at another woman but Travilla.

But how unlike the fairy-like Travilla was the worldly
Andreya!

'Will you take artichokes, Miss Garner?'

'Yes, please.' Lauri half turned and saw his profile
etched falcon-like in the lamplight. Andreya would not
be pleased when she heard about this supper *à deux*.

'You are sitting there very quiet.' He came and set a small table in front of the sofa where she sat.

'I am quiet when I'm pleased with my surroundings,' she smiled. 'Like a cat, I suppose.'

He quizzed her face with his keen dark eyes, and she saw a little smile in them, as if it pleased him that she liked his retreat, with its rich but sombre colours, its air of quiet seclusion.

'If I had a tower like this, *signor*,' she said impulsively, 'I should never want to leave it.'

'It might then become a prison instead of a quiet haven.' He went to the sideboard, and returned with a bowl of salad and white meat on a silver plate. 'One needs contact with the world in order to appreciate more fully the joys of retreat.'

'I suppose you're right.' She watched him arranging the food on the sofa table, and it shook her a little that this was actually her stern, dark master who munched an olive and told her to help herself to the fare while he poured the wine. Colour stole into her cheeks as she realized that she had sat here and let him wait on her.

'You must think me a lazy cat,' she said in confusion.

'I think you are young and rather shy.' The cork of the wine bottle popped and he filled a pair of wine glasses on twisted stems. 'This wine is known as Raingold. Do you like wine, *signorina*?'

'Mmmm, this is delicious.' Then catching his smile, she added out of bravado : 'I've had wine before, you know.'

'Of course.' He sat down beside her and helped himself to artichokes. 'I forgot that young Lonza has taken part of your education in hand. You must try some of this sauce with your salad.'

'Thank you.' She accepted a little of the spicy Italian

sauce, and through her lashes watched him deflowering the fawn-shot artichokes on his plate. He devoured the hearts with appetite, and broke amber-crusted bread in lean hands that were made to handle a rapier . . . or subdue a woman.

Beware! She ducked her head to her plate as he applied his table napkin to his lips and quizzed her profile over the rim of his wine goblet. 'Old wine must be enjoyed slowly,' he said. 'Do you like these goblets, *signorina*? They have been in my family for hundreds of years, and it is a thought to marvel at that we touch our lips to rims that have known the lips of men and women of the past. Does the idea intrigue you, Miss Garner? Or do you find it a little sad that old wine glasses should outlast the people who pledged their devotion over these silver rims?'

She fingered the twisted stem of her wine glass, and a terrible wonderment gripped her. To think that such fragility had outlasted the strength and arrogance of the Falcone di Cortes from whom the man beside her had sprung! She met the Titian directness of his eyes, dropped her glance to the shoulders that had a firm strength under stone-grey suiting. For the first time he seemed very human to her; a man who was as much at the mercy of life as she was.

'Have I frightened you?' He touched a finger to her chin and made her look at him. 'I forget that I am older and more resigned to the facts of life; that for each caress of the sun we must take three lashes of the whip.'

' "Life is a loom, weaving illusion",' she murmured. 'I've accepted that, so I can't be such a child, *signor*.'

He smiled and she saw the lines of character in his face, and was very aware for a moment of the charm of an amused male. 'Eat your chicken, *pepita*, then we will break the wishbone together.' He indicated the small triangular bone on the edge of the silver plate. 'Are those of the Land of Angels as superstitious as Venetians?'

'Country people are.' She broke into her throaty chuckle. 'Do you truly think Britain a land of angels?'

'Let us say devil-angels,' he smiled. 'The British people and the Venetians are both mercantile and artistic; alike in their pride and history. I also believe that the British are far more volatile in their emotions than they appear on the surface. Their air of coolness is a cloak for shyness – what, after all, is more impenetrable than shyness?'

A pair of dark eyes in a lean, Venetian face, she thought swiftly. 'I can't say I've ever heard a London taxi-driver serenading his customer,' she chuckled. 'Wouldn't it be funny to hear a romantic ballad issuing from the cabin of a taxi-cab?'

'I allow that our Venetian atmosphere is more conducive to romance.' He sat back against the tapestry of the sofa and the light of a nearby lamp played over the lower part of his face, leaving his eyes to glitter a little, as through a mask.

'Have you yet been serenaded in a gondola, Miss Garner?'

The question shook her a little, because a certain coolness had crept into his voice; a hint of displeasure, a return to formality. He had already guessed that last night, when she should have been sitting at his dining-table, she had been enjoying one of the most romantic joys Venice could offer.

'Yes,' she admitted. 'I – I thought it a charming experience.'

'For Lonza it must have been even more charming,'

drawled Maxim. 'Did he take advantage of the occasion to quote Musset?'

'Why should he do so?' Maxim's change of mood from charming host to sardonic inquisitor was disquieting; it made Lauri wonder if he had meant all along to chasten her for not putting herself on show last night for his friend the Contessa.

'According to Musset, a man and a woman have not explored all the mysteries of love until they have been alone together in a gondola.' Maxim made a steeple of his fingers, and the falcon-crest on his ring caught the lamplight and shimmered . . . as though with the lightning that the falcon held.

'Do you imagine that I'm exploring the mysteries of love with Michael?' Lauri exclaimed. 'Do you think that's all a girl thinks about when she goes out with a man?'

'No,' he shook his head very deliberately, 'I don't imagine it is all you think about, Miss Garner, but as I have pointed out to you before, Lonza is probably one of the most attractive dancers of this day and age. He has personality – and persistence, and you are a very young English girl whom I am responsible for.'

'I'm almost eighteen, *signor*,' she said with dignity, 'and I can assure you that I know how to take care of myself. I don't need a guardian – '

'All the same you have got one.' He leant forward and she was caught by his gaze like a pin drawn to steel. He studied her with a kind of ruthless deliberation. 'Innocence has little to do with age, child. It is a state of heart and spirit, a quality to be guarded by a detached friend until he feels you are ready for a deeper, more important relationship.'

'You mean I must await your permission to fall in

love?' She was all eyes and indignation in that moment. 'It really is true, isn't it? You really do expect a dancer to be your bondmaid. To bow to your commands, to dance at your direction only, to let you mould her as Pygmalion moulded his perfect woman. Only you want a perfect dancer – another Travilla !'

He didn't confirm or deny what she said. He merely rose from the sofa and went over to the sideboard, where he plugged in an electric coffee-percolator. The force of his silence weighed on Lauri, and she shrank down among the cushions of the sofa as though she wanted to hide herself from the wrath which she felt sure was brewing with the coffee.

'You flatter yourself, Miss Garner,' a spoon tinkled in a saucer, 'if you imagine that I see you as another Travilla. Is it possible that you imagine such a thing?'

'You know I don't.' She caught at a cushion and cuddled it against her like a shield. 'I even doubt my ability to perform on a stage as a member of your *corps de ballet*.'

'I share your doubts,' he said with cruel frankness. 'Will you take black or white coffee?'

'Black – please.'

The aroma of the coffee filled the room as he poured it out, and he was beside her with the little filigree cups before she could set aside the cushion she was holding. He looked down at her with glints of speculation in his eyes. 'I wonder what you would do if I suggested that you understudy Andreya in the role of Giselle,' he murmured.

'You're joking, of course, *signor*.' But was he? Her eyes searched his face, and she didn't know how pleading her eyes were. 'You have just said that you doubt my abilities.'

'Not your abilities – and do take your coffee before I spill some of it over that attractive dress.'

She took the cup and saucer, and eyed him warily. He didn't sit down beside her, as before, but went and settled himself in a big wing-backed chair facing her. He stirred his coffee, and Lauri was conscious of his lean and powerful grace of body, his air of being in command of every situation.

'There is much to be learned from a role like Giselle, and you need not fear that you will be called upon to dance it.' His eyes mocked her across the rim of his black and gold coffee cup. 'Andreya is rarely ill, but it may help you to gain confidence to learn so varied a role.'

'What will Andreya say?' The words broke from Lauri. 'She doesn't like me very much – '

'Which will make it all the more unlikely of her to fall victim to a mishap that would mean putting you in her place.' His smile had a diablerie about it. 'Andreya is your assurance, child, that you will not be called upon to dance Giselle at a moment's notice.'

The very idea sent a cold shiver through Lauri, which she assuaged with the dark Italian coffee. 'I should let you down, and you would be furious,' she said tensely. 'Your aim is perfection, and the only dancers who give it are those who love nothing else, or those who are inspired by a man they love.'

'And you fall into neither category, is that it, Miss Garner?' He took a cigar from his case and clipped the end deliberately and evenly. He lit up and the aromatic smoke drifted over towards Lauri. 'Must I assume that I waste my time and knowledge on a girl who would sooner be a secretary, let us say, than a dancer?'

'A need for security is no joke.' Her voice shook a little

for when he narrowed his eyes and held that cigar
clamped between his teeth he looked rather dangerous.
'I – I have no sense of security when I dance, *signor*. I try
to overcome the shadow that always seems to dance at
my heels, but sometimes it's more than a shadow. It
grabs at my ankles and I go stiff, or I stumble. You've
seen it happen!'

'Yes,' his eyes pierced her through the smoke of his
cigar, 'and I think it is self-induced, a possible means
of escape from dancing into the more ordinary life which
you feel will give you security.'

'I don't make it happen,' her nostrils flared with
shock at the idea. 'How can you say that?'

'Our deeper emotions have more control over our
actions that we realize, *signorina*. Our pains, and our
pleasures, have long memories. No matter how far we
run from pain, it pursues us. No matter how we long
for what would please us, it eludes. It is only when we
stand firm and face our furies that we conquer them.'

He smiled, with that quick charm that conquered.
'I promised to show you some things of Travilla's which
I keep from love, and for luck. Would you like to see
them?'

'Very much, *signor*.'

'I will fetch them. Please excuse me for one moment.'

He strode from the room, and Lauri sank back against
the cushions of the sofa with closed eyes. Maxim Falcone
di Corte was a formidable man to argue with; he left
one defenceless, and curiously weak. She let the momen-
tary peace of the room seep into her, and wondered if
he was as merciless when it came to love.

He returned, cigar in mouth, carrying a small carved
chest with painted panels. He set it down on the sofa
and Lauri saw how delightful the panels were. Zeus

being bound by the Olympians. Clotho spinning the threads of life. Poseidon, the sea-god, racing over the waves in his chariot. Greca with her unicorn.

Maxim touched the little twisted horn of the unicorn and the lid of the chest sprang open. Lauri caught her breath, her legs curled beneath her as he showed her his treasured mementos. A black lace domino that Travilla had worn at a masked ball, which he held for a moment against Lauri's face. A scarlet fan that had fluttered in a small hand. Amber beads with a little cross attached. A pair of satin dancing slippers with little scarlet heels.

'Try them on,' Maxim said, and the next moment he knelt down on the carpet, took Lauri's right foot in his hand and replaced her shoe with one of Travilla's. 'Now the other,' he coaxed.

She let him have his way, feeling the light brush of his fingers and their firmer grip as he drew her to her feet. 'Do they fit?' he asked. 'Try a few steps in them.'

As though under his spell she took a few steps in the shoes, then she turned to face him, her dress of rowan red throwing into relief her slender neck, her wing of dark hair, the fine unpowdered texture of her skin, and the dusky gold of her eyes.

'You look as though Dante created you for his poem.' Maxim studied her with a remote kind of interest. 'How does it feel to stand in Travilla's shoes?'

Lauri felt the quick beat of her pulse at his words.

'A little alarming,' she said, and escaped from his eyes by bending to remove the shoes. She brought them to him and was glad when he put them away without any further comment.

'You must see this, *signorina*.' He unveiled carefully a jewelled goblet with a silver lid. 'This is a marriage

goblet of the sixteenth century, that it is lidded makes
it a symbol of the human heart. Do you wish to hold it?'

She nodded and took it gently into her hands. It was
very lovely and she saw at once the Latin inscription
carved upon the lid. 'What do the words mean, *signor*?'
she asked.

He bent his dark head and she breathed the smoke of
his cigar as he traced the lettering with his fingertip.
' "Flee what is sweet, if it can turn to bitterness",' he
translated. 'It no doubt implies that two people should
take care that what they feel is true love; the other kind
can turn bitter, and marriage in Italy is for life.'

For life, she thought. How sweet, how secure, if
indeed the sweetness grew out of true love.

Maxim shrouded the marriage goblet in its veil once
more, to lie in hiding until the time came for him and
his bride to drink from it their pledge to love each other
... for life.

He closed the lid of the chest and the action had a
finality about it. Lauri slipped her feet into her shoes,
and then gave a little shiver as she felt his fingers close
over her shoulder. She glanced up at him and he was
closer than she realized, her red velvet clinging against
his grey suiting. She would have drawn away, but he
took her squarely by the shoulders and held her in front
of him.

'Tomorrow we begin work together on *Giselle*,' he
said. 'We will be working alone, so there will be no need
to tell anyone that I am teaching you the role.'

By 'anyone' he meant Andreya. For Andreya's sake
he wished to be secretive, and for her own sake Lauri
was glad to fall in with the suggestion.

'*Chi tace consente?*' he murmured.

'Of course I consent, *signor*.'

'*Buono.*' His smile etched lines beside his dark eyes.
'You begin to understand a little Italian. Soon you must
begin to speak it. It is convenient for a dancer to have
several languages at her command, for the world is wide
and the di Corte Company travels far.'

'You expect me to stay with the di Corte Company,
signor? What if I stumble on the stage of the Fenice
when we begin the new season?'

'I forbid you to even think about it.' His fingers
tightened warningly, sending little currents through the
bones of her shoulders. There was a smouldering way
back in his eyes, like the shadow of flame in the depths
of a forge. 'Tonight you stood in Travilla's shoes . . .
remember it and don't let her down.'

He let her go, and added crisply that he would escort
her to the foot of the tower steps. 'But first,' he bent to
their supper table and took from the edge of the silver
plate the little wishbone from the chicken they had
shared, 'we must break this and see who will get the
wish.'

They each hooked a little finger about the jointed
bone, and though Lauri did not feel him pull on it, he
held the wishing end when the bone broke in two.

She smiled, and wondered what sort of wish a man
like Maxim di Corte made. Success for the new season
that commenced in six weeks' time?

Six weeks . . . they would pass all too soon, and for
the first time Lauri would dance in front of a theatre
audience. Perhaps when the night drew near for that
debut at the Fenice, the lovely old Venetian theatre
on the water, Aunt Pat might manage to come to Venice
to lend her support to the occasion.

'You wear a little smile as though you also have made
a wish.' Maxim glanced at her as they arrived at the

foot of the tower steps, where a lamp in a wall niche cast subtle shadows over his face and intensified his look of another century.

'Girls are always wishing for things.' Lauri met his eyes that could be kind but were more often keen; deep-set eyes that concealed far more than they revealed. 'Thank you for giving me supper in your tower, *signor*. I enjoyed the experience.'

'It was pleasant for me to have your company, *signorina*,' he said formally. 'Now hurry indoors to your bed. *Buona notte.*'

'*Buona notte, signor.*'

She entered the *palazzo* by a door leading from the tower, and as she crossed to the stairs the hall clock began to strike. She counted the strokes made by the bronze figure on top of the clock, and was halfway to the gallery when she experienced again that chilly feeling that she was being watched. It made her quicken her footsteps, and once inside her room she stood with her back to the door in a defensive attitude. Her fingers felt for the key and turned it quickly . . . but she couldn't lock out of her mind the uneasy conviction that someone had stood in the half-dark of the hall, watching her enter the *palazzo* through Maxim di Corte's private door.

CHAPTER SEVEN

Maxim walked behind her, holding her arms, curving them and directing her. 'Move from the hips,' he commanded. 'It is from the hips that a woman conveys her awareness of her femininity, and at this point in the ballet, remember, you are a carefree young girl in love. A peasant girl who knows that love is not coy but joyful. *Bene*. Good, now I will watch while you dance your thoughts of your young man – whom you think of as a peasant. You do not yet know that he is a prince in disguise.'

He went and seated himself in the big window recess of their practice room, which was at the rear of the *palazzo*. It overlooked the walled garden, and was secluded and spacious, with an angle at the far end.

Now that Lauri was under his direct observation she grew nervous and a quiver spoiled the line of her *port de bras*; the all-important supple line from shoulders to fingertips.

'You are nervous', he thundered. 'Of course you are, for nerves are part of a dancer's equipment. Accept them, child, as you accept your hair, your eyes and the little mole on your temple . . . and then forget them.'

'It's easy enough for you to talk', she retorted, her head bent as she rubbed her dancing slippers in the rosin box. 'You have no nerves.'

'Which is just as well when I am dealing with you.' His smile was narrow and dangerous. 'You might really do better to take up typing, though I believe your hands would be just as clumsy as your feet.'

'Thank you,' she said, and fired by his sarcasm she performed a twinkling chain of *petite batterie*.

'Must I always be angry with you to make you dance?' He laughed mockingly. 'Now go to the far end of the room, which we will regard as the wings of a stage, and begin to dance for me – I am still in a rage, remember – your love for Loys, whom you think of as your peasant sweetheart.'

Lauri stood there in that angle of the room that hid her from him, and let herself think swiftly of Giselle, the girl who was ready to die for love if she couldn't live for it. She had always loved the ballet, but she couldn't have told anyone how much it was taking hold of her since Maxim had started to take her, morning by morning, through its many movements and moods.

She closed her eyes, then ran forward as though out of the door of Giselle's tiny cottage. She gave a soft high spring and curved her arms as though to embrace the thought of her sweetheart, then she retreated backwards on the very points of her toes, alarmed in the face of love as girls are.

At the end of her solo, Maxim held out a hand to her and she went to him and gave him her hand. 'Do you see how easy and natural it is when you forget yourself?' he murmured.

She nodded, and felt the fascination of his smile to the marrow of her bones.

'You like *Giselle*, eh? You feel the poetry and power of the story? That must mean that you are a romantic, Miss Garner.'

'I suppose I am,' she admitted. 'Aren't most women?'

'Yes, most women dream, but have to put reality first.' He brushed a teasing kiss across her wrist, and even as she stood tingling from the shock, added crisply : 'Tomorrow I take you to hear the choir of San Marco, one of the most glorious in Italy. A dancer should have an affinity with great music, and I am curious to see your reaction to the choir. You have not yet been to hear it?'

She shook her head. 'I had heard about it, of course.'

'I think that romantic heart of yours will be moved by it.' He rose lazily to his feet and turned his gaze upon the walled garden, where a bird was perched on the head of a broken-nosed statue. 'After our visit to San Marco, I am taking you to lunch at the Villa Nora with the Contessa Riffini. She was a great friend of Travilla's and will tell you all about the Italian ballets of some years ago. They were colourful pageants rather than the consecutive stories we tell today.'

It was all arranged, Lauri realized. If she had made a previous arrangement, then it would have to be set on one side.

He turned abruptly to face her, as though he sensed what was going through her mind. 'I am sure you realize that you are here in Venice not on vacation but to work,' he said crisply. 'No doubt you have made plans for tomorrow, but Lonza will have to be let down as I was let down the other evening.'

'Of course, *signor*.' She winced from the cutting edge to his voice. 'I do realize that work comes before – pleasure.'

He took that one with a thin, dangerous smile, and Lauri was relieved when he glanced at his wristwatch and said it was time she joined the others for the coffee break.

She was at the door when it opened with a suddenness that made her leap backwards. Hands caught at her arms and she was held against the hardness of Maxim's chest as Andreya came sweeping into the practice room.

Tension leapt like a flame as the ballerina stared at Lauri, who couldn't move a muscle of her body in her black leotard. Her heart thudded. She took like a shield the arrows that leapt from Andreya's eyes.

'What are you rehearsing, Max?' Andreya looked sharply at his tousled hair, and his white shirt open at the throat. 'A little cradle-snatching?'

'Not quite,' he said, and for a heart-stopping moment Lauri thought he was going to say outright that he was teaching her the role of Giselle. She knew he was annoyed; she could feel it in the grip of his hands and in the tenseness of his body. 'I am not the sort to feel amorous about infants, and Miss Garner will tell you herself, Lydia, that she finds me a taskmaster from whom she was hurrying away when you almost thrust the door in her face.'

'Really?' Andreya's long fingers plucked at the ruby of her antique poison-ring. 'You should be flattered, my girl, to receive personal instruction from Max. No doubt he thinks you a slow learner who might spoil the precision of the *corps de ballet* – not a thing, you know, is ever allowed to mar an evening of di Corte ballet.'

Colour stung Lauri's cheeks, and she wished fiercely that she was brilliant and that Maxim would say so.

'You are right, Lydia, I allow nothing to spoil a performance by the di Corte Company.' He gave Lauri a lazy little push away from him, towards the door. 'In that I am more ruthless than in anything else.'

'You are ruthless about love as well, Max. You will not give in to your feelings until you feel it is right to do so. . . .' Lauri caught this remark just before she closed the door and shut Andreya in with him. She hurried away, and was glad to enter the hall where coffee was being served to the dancers, along with cheese and ham rolls. Michael held up two mugs of coffee and indicated that he wished to share the break with her. She knew he was fond of cheese and took him over a couple of rolls. They sat side by side on the stairs, and he tossed his cardigan around her shoulders.

'You look a trifle tortured, pet.' He bit into a roll and eyed her with concern. 'Maxim can be a demon in the practice room, so I gather he has been putting you through the mill and grinding you down into small pieces. Don't let him grind too hard, Nijinka. I think you are a very good dancer, despite what Andreya says.'

'What does Madame Andreya say?' Lauri spoke tartly, and felt real dislike of another human being for the first time in her life.

'She says that Maxim will dismiss you because you are too nervous to be a real professional. You are a nervous little thing, Lauri,' he gave her a curious but affectionate glance. 'You should be proud to have talent, and not act like a shy little mouse. A cat is always ready to pounce on a mouse.'

Lauri sipped at her coffee and supposed, wryly, that he was right. Andreya did pounce at every opportunity, and right in front of Maxim, as though she was so sure of him that she didn't have to pretend to be nicer than she was. But then he was very worldly and adult, and had more or less said that love was too basic to be wrapped in the veils of illusion.

'What have you been doing all the morning?' she asked Michael.

'Practising, practising!' He gave a sigh followed by an exaggerated groan. 'It feels good to be relaxing with you, pet.'

'Pet mouse?' She gave her throaty little laugh. 'What

have you been practising? I saw Madame Andreya a
while ago dressed in street clothes, so I gather you have
not been working with her.'

'I have been working on my solo, the Dance of Devils-
hoof.' He winked at her. 'You will love me as a gipsy
bandit.'

'The dance sounds exciting.' Lauri eyed him with the
old schoolgirlish admiration, and she was struck anew
by the strangeness of events. One moment she had been
a ballet pupil living peacefully with her aunt at Downhollow ... and the next a tall, dark *maître de ballet*
strode into her life and carried her off to his Venetian
palace to be, quite literally, his bondmaid, his slave of
the dance. ...

'One moment your thoughts are all for me, then the
next a shadow erases them.' Michael followed the fragile
line of her profile with his fingertip. 'What troubles you,
little mouse? Surely by now we are friends enough for
the sharing of a – secret?'

She gave a little shiver at the word and drew his cardigan closer about her. 'I was just thinking what a com-
plex person the Director is, the way he shields himself
behind a mask, almost, the moment you stop dancing
for him.'

'If he makes an artist of you, what does all the rest
matter?'

'It matters, because I am pretty sure he wouldn't
waste a minute on me if I had no real dancing ability.'
She frowned at Michael, who was smiling as though at
a little oddity. 'Don't you ever wonder if he has
ever spared time to notice people as human beings
rather than puppets, or artistic creations he has
moulded?'

'*Pauvre enfant*, you think too much.' Michael was

lazily amused, then all at once on the alert. 'Do you mean you want to be noticed by him – as a girl?'

'Good heavens, no !' She looked alarmed by the idea.

'Women have been known to love him,' Michael said wickedly. 'But he, of course, is a true falcon. All the Falcone di Cortes have been men who attached themselves to one person for life . . . and we both know the name of the lady to whom Maxim appears to be attached.'

Lauri nodded and thought of Andreya in the street suit cut perfectly to the sleek lines of her figure. She thought of her on-stage, supreme in certain roles, beautiful in a terrifying, Ellida-like fashion.

A man would have to be stronger than the need for warmth and affection to love a woman like Andreya . . . and such strength struck Lauri as inhuman.

'There are deep-burning fires in him that melt the iron now and again.' Michael's breath brushed her ear. 'What is Maxim teaching you? I have danced *Lurline* with you and I know you have gone beyond the pupil stage. I think you could dance a major role – '

'No !' Her face went white. 'I am not ready for anything like that. It means nothing that Signor di Corte is teaching me the role of – '

There she broke off, aghast. Michael's eyes glittered and he caught at her hand. 'Which role?' He was breathing with excitement. 'You can tell me, Lauri. I don't like Andreya well enough to give away a secret that could hurt you.'

'Let go of my hand,' she pleaded. 'Bruno's class is about to begin and I must go.'

'I know which role Maxim is teaching you.' Michael spoke in a low, exultant voice. 'He wouldn't be able to

resist it when you look so much like – Lauri, we would
be the sensation of the season in *Giselle* together. I know
it, feel it! You are the right age for me, the right temperament – I am going to ask Maxim to let me have you
as a partner.'

'No, Michael.' She caught at his shoulder with her
free hand, and her face was only a few inches from his
as she pleaded with him. 'He would laugh at the idea,
and be terribly angry at the same time.'

'I have had confrontations with the *grand signor*
before this.' Michael was looking reckless, his hair in
damp disorder from a morning of strenuous practice,
his black sweater slashed open to the waist. 'Lauri, little
mouse with the big eyes, *I must have you.*'

The words rang out in the silence that had followed
the dispersal of the other dancers, but the hall wasn't
entirely empty. A tall figure was crossing towards the
door that led to the *palazzo* tower. He paused and
turned his gaze upon the couple on the stairs – his
gaze was so direct that to evade it was impossible, and
after he had gone on his way, Lauri still felt him looking
right through her. She still saw his compressed lips, his
haughty nose, and the chin like a piece of Italian marble
that had got chipped in the centre.

'Michael, do you think he heard us?' she whispered.

'What of it? He will now be forewarned about what
I am going to ask him.'

'You can't.' The whiteness of her face was very notice-
able in contrast to her black leotard. 'I – I shall run away
if you do. I couldn't bear to stay here with Signor di
Corte thinking I am after a role that belongs to
Andreya.'

'I think it belongs to you,' Michael said obstinately.
'Why should you not be given a chance to dance it?

Why is he teaching you the role if he does not intend you to dance it?'

'He says that I need to gain confidence, and the diversity of the role is good practice for me.'

'Why all the secrecy?' Michael demanded.

'You know Andreya.' Lauri shrugged, and still felt as though a cold fist had taken hold of her heart. 'Michael, promise not to say anything. He'll think that I go running to you with – with tales.'

'Every little mouse must have a bolt-hole.' Michael studied her in some perplexity. 'Would you squeak if I kissed you on the neck?'

At once she leapt to her feet, supple as a switch and as ready to strike. He laughed up at her, with a glinting male light in his eyes. 'What is it to be?' he mocked. 'A kiss on the neck – but not right now – or a talk with Maxim?'

'I won't be blackmailed,' she gasped.

'All right,' he rose to his feet with animal grace and took a couple of steps in the direction of Maxim's private door. Lauri hesitated only long enough to visualize Maxim's angry frown.

'You win,' she said, with a flash of temper. 'And I hate you for it.'

He swung round to face her, a lean dark pagan with the silent tread of a puma. As he drew near, she backed against the baluster of the stairs. 'You're outrageous,' she said.

'But also a rather good dancer, and I know you like that about me.' He grinned down at her. 'Come, everyone has a redeeming quality and mine is honesty. You have a rare enchantment, if you did but know it.'

'You have a lot of experience, Mr. Lonza, and I intrigue you for no other reason than that I am a new member of the di Corte Company, and I do not run after you.'

'"Do I not see a heart naturally furnished with wings?".' He quoted Keats, and his smile was curiously tender. 'Someone once said of romance that it is bitter-sweet wine, a ravishing sadness, a dancing shape waiting to waylay a man. Methinks I am waylaid, little mouse who thinks too much.'

'I think I should be on my way to class,' she said firmly.

'And when do I collect my forfeit?' As he took his cardigan from around her shoulders, his fingertips brushed the nape of her neck. 'Tomorrow, when I take you to see the House of Gold on the Grand Canal?'

'Michael,' she pressed a hand against her throat, 'I – I can't come with you tomorrow.'

'Why not?' There was a sudden menacing stillness about him.

'Signor di Corte has made other arrangements for me. You know his high-handed way of doing things – I'm to hear the choir of San Marco, and afterwards he's taking me to meet the Contessa Riffini. I suppose he feels I need educating in the arts.'

'Is this educational outing to be a threesome?' Michael spoke sarcastically. 'It should be fun, with Maxim cramming you with culture, and Andreya hating you because you are sweet seventeen.'

'*Michael!*' She looked so cast down that in an instant he was laughing and pulling her hair.

'I am keeping you from your class, you poor child. Have supper with me tonight to make up for tomorrow?'

She nodded, and then ran to her class as though pursued.

Sunday at the *palazzo* was always a lazy day. And the bronze music of the many church bells seemed to add to the air of peace and rest.

Lauri stood listening to the bells over the water as Maxim di Corte paid the gondolier who had brought them to the steps of the San Marco Piazza. Then he joined her and they walked among the pigeons to the sculptured entrance of the great Byzantine church.

The clear spring air etched in classic outline the spires and domes, about which the pigeons fluttered like doves of peace.

There was a barbaric majesty about the great golden church, and Lauri's heart seemed to open to the beauty, then to close and hold it within her.

'All the romantic mythology of Venice is blended in that one building,' Maxim said to her, and when she glanced at him the sun on his hair made it gleam like a falcon's wing.

She smiled, slim and barely reaching to the shoulder of his pin-check suit in her own Sunday suit the colour of wood violets. What a relief that Andreya was not with them; her hostile presence would have spoiled Lauri's pleasure in the bronze pealing of bells, the spring sunshine, and the bustling by of nuns in immense coifs, shepherding a brood of convent pupils.

As they entered San Marco, a golden twilight seemed to enclose them, and through it the mosaic-lined cupolas glowed with colour and flashes of gold. Each told a Bible story. Adam and Eve, and their Paradise Lost. Noah and the animals of the Ark. Moses performing one of his God-given miracles.

The floors were also mosaic-tiled. There were marble columns, cloisters and Gothic arches. More cupolas, and galleries; stone angels and prophets outlined by the colours of the great rose windows.

The atmosphere was dusky, oriental, mystical.

Lauri knew that she would never forget that service at San Marco, the flicker of candle flames, and the glorious echo made by the choir music. It moved her unbearably, and when at last she followed Maxim out into the bright sunlight of the Piazza, she felt a dampness on her lashes and glanced away quickly when he looked at her.

'Have you seen the campanile from the balcony of the lantern tower?' he asked.

She shook her head, and they went up in a lift with other visitors to San Marco, and Maxim took her to a gallery and they gazed down upon the gold-washed domes, the statues of the winged lion of St. Mark, and St. Theodore with his crocodile, mounted on gigantic columns, the people and pigeons mingling below in the immense square, and the vista of sea-green beyond the campanile.

'Casanova might have stood here with his lady of the moment, admiring this very view,' Maxim smiled. 'Venice, the most unchanging city in the world, a dream and yet a reality.'

Lauri watched him touch with a lean hand the haunch of one of the bronze horses, fashioned long ago in Athens, and once a part of the Triumphal Arch of Nero.

And then from a nearby clock tower, two metal Moorish figures struck the hour. As the strokes echoed, pigeons fluttered. Maxim's lean hand found Lauri's elbow and he said they must be on their way to the Villa Nora, which was situated on one of the Laguna islands.

The Contessa's privately owned gondola awaited them at the steps leading down from the Piazza, a big peaked vessel with a pair of rowers dressed in smart dark livery. Lauri sank back against the fringed black cushions of her seat, and for a moment Maxim loomed dark above her and she was reminded vividly of her evening alone with him in his tower, when he had made her confess to having been serenaded in a gondola with Michael.

He sat down facing her, and she thought how strange it was to be sharing a gondola with him. As the graceful black boat slid away into the green water of the lagoon, an awareness of him as a man rather than a master came to her. He could be very kind in his aloof fashion, and she had glimpsed how vulnerable he was in his love of beauty. His gaze was on the medieval façade of the Basilica as they drew away from it, and she had never seen him look so gentle.

'Did I react to the choir as you hoped, *signor*?' she asked with a smile.

'Your reaction was very agreeable.' He returned her smile. 'Young people are not easy to please, and the things that delight an older palate are sometimes dull to a younger one.'

'You are not dull,' she said, and then glanced away from him in some confusion and took in the Venetian boats that sailed on the lagoon, their bows painted with strange magical designs, their sails rust-brown against the blue-green of sky and water.

'Oh, look!' She pointed to a small flotilla of gondolas that went by, bright with flowers and merrymakers. Music came across the water, and laughter.

'A Venetian wedding party,' Maxim told her.

'How lovely', she murmured, 'to go to your wedding in a gondola. It's so picturesque and gay.'

'You child,' he said, and shielded the flame of his lighter from the lagoon breeze as he lit a cigarette. 'You should get on well with the Contessa, who remains as young at heart as a girl. Her villa is like something wafted on a magic carpet from the orient; it stands exotic as Scheherezade's pavilion on the shores of the island. Her indulgent husband had it built for her many years ago as a summer residence, and at present she has her goddaughter staying with her. Venetia is a widow. Her story is a sad one, and the Contessa fears that she will never recover from the double loss of her husband and her small son of three.'

His glance probed Lauri's sensitive face. 'Venetia adored her husband,' he said quietly, 'and their son was the crown on that happiness. Their home was on the outskirts of Florence, in the direct path of those terrible floods of last year. Venetia is a sculptress of small child-figures and animals, and she had gone to Rome where an exhibition of her work was being arranged. She was away from home the night the flood waters broke through their barrier and destroyed half the city . . . and swept her husband and child out of her life for ever.'

'How *awful*!' Lauri whispered.

'Even more so because Venetia is a fine and lovely girl.' He drew hard on his cigarette, and his eyes were shadowed by his dark brows. 'Her life has been cruelly shattered, and she shows little interest in continuing with her work. She spends hours by herself, just looking at the river – the river that took her husband and the little one.'

'Would it not be best for the Contessa to take her into the country?' Lauri asked. 'You say the villa is on the shores of the island – '

'Devils pursue, Miss Garner. They are not driven away if we run from them . . . you realize now why I wished you to meet my friends, Venetia in particular?'

'Yes, because of my parents,' she said quietly. 'I learned to live without them, *signor*, but those you love are special people and it never really stops hurting that something should hurt them. What happens is that a skin grows over your grief, shielding it from other people's impatience.'

Maxim's eyes seemed to harden when she said that. 'You think I am impatient with you?' he demanded.

She nodded and looked away from his unnerving frown. 'Sometimes you – you seem to be.'

'You think I don't understand what it means to love someone, and to be hurt? You think I am made of stone?' The questions lashed at her, like cold spray over the bows of the gondola.

She pulled her gaze from the glimmer of the sea, through which the gondola was cutting towards the deeper green of an island. She looked at Maxim and saw that his face was as if cut in stone. 'Your strength of will is greater than other people's,' she said. 'I am not saying that your understanding is less.'

'Thank you,' he said with irony. 'I take it that in your estimation people should give way to their feelings?'

'No – you twist my words –'

'Perhaps a little,' he admitted, 'but it is unwise to provoke a man by implying that he has no feelings . . . he might be tempted to prove you wrong.'

Her eyes met his, wildly.

'What would you do then?' he mocked. 'Gondoliers take no notice when a man puts his arms around a woman in a gondola. They would merely look the other way – if I kissed you.'

'But you wouldn't!' She drew back against the black gondola cushions and looked very much a shrinking violet in that moment.

His eyes flicked her hair, the tiny mole at her temple, the pulse in her throat. His face was dark, unreadable, then with a laugh of arrant mockery he sat back in his seat and watched lazily as the gondoliers rowed them to the landing-stage of the island.

A stepped terrace rose above the shore, and the sun was bright on the white walls of the Villa Nora.

CHAPTER EIGHT

LAURI turned to look at the view beyond the terrace, and her eyes sparkled like the sea.

Then with renewed delight she looked at the villa, with its upward twining loggias of stucco like thick white lace. She heard the sea whispering, and the wild bees humming in the cloaks of wallflowers, double-flowering, sweet-scented masses of cream on apricot and beige on rose.

'Do you like the villa?' Maxim asked.

'It does have a look of the Arabian Nights about it,' she replied, and when she glanced at him she saw how proud and dark he looked, sculptured against the blue-green seascape, the colourful mass of flowers, and the terrace guard that sloped upwards beside the wide steps. The white wall was fretted along its surface, with arabesques cut deeply in the stucco.

He lounged against the ornamental wall, and with the sun behind him his eyes were masked, while she stood in the full play of light. 'This place also has a most disturbing effect on me,' he said, 'but perhaps the heat of the sun melts my hard feelings, eh?'

He was goading her, she knew that, but when she saw the glimmer of his teeth in a mocking smile she couldn't resist the impulse to answer the challenge in his words and his smile.

'People compare you to a falcon because of your family crest and background,' she said, 'but isn't it a fact, *signor*, that the falcon disdains affection and takes the hearts of the small, flashing birds in the sky?'

A silence stretched between them, and her heartbeats seemer louder than the sea whispers and the bees humming.

'The small, flashing birds are my dancers, I take it, of whom I demand everything without giving an atom of my own heart?' He moved towards her, so quickly that she put up a hand as though to fend him off. 'You little fool, you don't know a thing about me!'

He walked on ahead of her, and above the clamour of her heart she heard him hail someone. She shielded her eyes with her hand and saw a woman standing at the top of the steps, a slim figure in black with hair that blew in the breeze off the sea and had a hint of dark flame in it.

The woman was young and Lauri guessed from the black she wore that she was Venetia, about whom he had spoken so gently.

Maxim gazed long at Venetia, and as Lauri drew near to them he took the young woman's hands into his as though they were flowers. He carried them to his lips, and there was about the gesture a tender gallantry that thrilled through Lauri like a pain. The couple spoke together in low tones, then he turned to Lauri and beckoned her to him with an imperious gesture.

'This is my young protégée, Venetia.' The smile he gave the young widow was a brilliant mingling of dark eyes and white teeth. The look he gave Lauri was quick and cool, nor did his voice linger warmly on her name when he introduced her.

'I am glad to meet you, Signorina Garner.' Venetia had a voice with a ghostly echo of warmth in it, her fine features were shadowed by sadness, and her eyes spoke eloquently of the suffering she still endured. Her eyes would be remarkable in animation, for they were the shade of blue seen in stained-glass windows, and strikingly framed by her dark auburn hair.

'Zena waits impatiently for you both in her "virgin's bower" as she calls the sun loggia.' Venetia gave Lauri a fleeting smile. 'Because of the clematis, you understand, which grows in profusion all over the loggia. I must warn you that the Contessa has a sharp wit, but please don't let her alarm you too much.'

Lauri smiled back at Venetia. 'I am quite used by now to being alarmed, *signora.*'

Venetia glanced at Maxim, who gave Lauri an ironical little bow. 'The child refers to me, Venetia,' he said. 'She considers me quite a taskmaster, and also has the effrontery to say I have no heart.'

'You said that to Max?' Venetia gazed at Lauri in some surprise. 'I have always found him the kindest of men.'

'Miss Garner will retort that you have never had to dance for me.' He flicked a mocking smile over Lauri's face, and as she gazed back at him little pieces of gold fell through the branches of the trees and seemed caught in her wide eyes.

'As an artist, Venetia, you see people as art forms both mythical and symbolic.' He gestured at Lauri in her woodsmoke suit, her hair a dark switch reaching to her heart. 'Of what does my protégée remind you?'

Venetia studied Lauri with those deep blue eyes that were so disturbing. 'Of an Aretino faun,' she said quietly. 'And now, Max, stop teasing her. If you do this all the time, then it is no wonder the poor girl thinks you unkind.'

'She thinks me a tyrant.' He laughed low in his throat, and stood aside so that the two girls could precede him along the path to the sun loggia. It was octagonal and surmounted by a cupola. Clematis vines clambered all over the white walls, and a fountain tinkled as they entered the little sun temple where the Contessa awaited them.

She sat in a fan-backed wicker chair, a little bee of a woman, carved out of ivory and held together with lace and bombazine. A white, blue-eyed cat sat on her lap, and she stroked the snowy fur with a tiny, jewelled hand. Her eyes were shrewd, inquisitive, and they flashed over Lauri as she gave her other hand to Maxim to be kissed.

'I notice you don't apologize for being late,' she said to him.

'A Venetian is never on time, you know that, Contessa.'

'Humph!' She looked at him, and her eyes sparkled like the gems encrusting her rings. 'You mean you never apologize for anything. A woman could wait an hour, or a lifetime, and never humble you.'

'What do you think would humble me?' he asked, a glitter of devilry in his eyes.

'You are a Falcone di Corte,' the Contessa said deliberately, 'fated to love one woman. You may find that you will have to humble yourself to her, Max.'

'Heaven forbid!' he laughed.

'On the contrary, Max, if heaven allows.'

He quirked an eyebrow, but when he made no reply the Contessa said wickedly, 'Ah, have I the king in checkmate?'

'No, I have a gambit that could surprise the queen,' he replied, 'but I am not prepared right now to show my hand.'

'Timidity, *amico caro*?' she mocked.

'Expediency, *signora*.' He swung smartly to face Lauri and held out his hand to her as though to a child. 'Come along, the Contessa won't bite you now she has had a go at my tough skin.'

Lauri took a nervous step forward and the warm steel of his fingers drew her right in front of the intimidating little woman in the great wicker chair. The jetty eyes played over her face, while the white cat rose on all fours and looked at her as well.

'Stroke him, go on,' the Contessa said. 'Minou likes the very young and the very old because he is wise like all cats.'

'He's beautiful,' Lauri smiled, and with her hand on the cat's silky white fur it was easier to withstand the scrutiny of his mistress.

'Beauty is irrelevant,' the Contessa said. 'If he were not wise and loyal I would not love him for his blue eyes alone. So you are Maxim's protégée? Do you like being his pupil of the dance? Or do you fight with him?'

Lauri met the Contessa's eyes and saw in them none of the awe which Maxim aroused in everyone else. To her, incredibly, he had been known from a baby.

'Does my question embarrass you?' the Contessa asked.

'You must remember, Zena, that Miss Garner is British,' Maxim said dryly.

'A reticent nation, to be sure. Venetia *mia*, will you pour our refreshments?' A servant in a white jacket had just carried in a tray and set it down on a wicker table in front of the fountain. There was a cool clink of ice against glass, and the sun poured warm through the arched openings of the loggia.

'Take off your jacket and be cooler,' the Contessa said to Lauri. 'Come, sit here beside me and we will talk.'

Lauri fumbled with the buttons of her jacket and as she withdrew her arms from the sleeves she felt Maxim take the jacket from her. She wore a sleeveless blouse and was suddenly conscious of how pale her skin was in contrast to his. Venetia gave her a grave smile and a long glass of fruit juice.

'Gin and vermouth for you, Max.' Venetia carried the drink to him, and as Lauri glanced over at them she was struck by the foil his darkness made for Venetia's auburn colouring. His gaze seemed to cover her, warm and sheltering.

'This is an unusual child, Max,' the Contessa remarked as he relaxed into a lounger beside the young widow. 'She has a strange quality of stillness, like a brook in a woodland. Most benign. You must let me have her for a companion if you fail to make a dancer of her.'

'I don't intend to fail,' he said, and his brows were drawn down like a visor over the eyes that were like black steel as they dwelt on Lauri. 'She will dance for me as I wish her to, then she will be free as a bird. Then she may choose to be someone's companion – but not yours, Zena.'

'And why not, may I ask?'

Lauri felt the probe of jetty eyes and wanted to retort that she wasn't a doll, a marionette to be given away when Maxim di Corte was tired of pulling her strings.

'I have an aunt in England,' she said, giving him a cool look. 'She wished me to try and find success as a dancer, and I came to Venice for her sake.'

'Do you like Venice?' Venetia asked in her gentle, hollow voice.

'It is very picturesque and unusual,' Lauri replied.

'But you miss England?'

'Yes – my home is there, and my aunt and I have always been very close.' A sudden wave of longing for the homely security of Aunt Pat's cottage swept over her. Dear Aunt Pat would be putting the Sunday joint in the oven, and the Sunday music programme would be on the radio. There would be cuckoos calling in the lanes of Downhollow, and catkins budding on the willows by the old millstream – it was unbearable, this ache in her heart for the simple things she loved, and the security she needed.

'So your aunt wishes you to be a success?'

Lauri glanced at the Contessa. 'She was in ballet herself as a girl, you see –'

'And one likes to please a loved one, eh?' The jetty eyes smiled shrewdly. 'That is the way of life, my child. We are all victims of the impulses of our hearts, but having lived a long and varied life I know that what makes it exciting and warm and enriching is this drive we have towards other people. This need to love, and to be loved. It may hurt us, and very often it does, but it is the very essence of living, and those who shield themselves from its abrasions are dull and lifeless people.'

'You mean, Contessa, that it is out in the world that we learn to face up to life?'

'Exactly so.' A jewelled hand patted Lauri's. 'If your aunt used her love for you only to protect you, then she would do you more harm than good. I am sure you have talent – Max would not waste his precious time on anything less – and the elusive magic, perhaps, that theatregoers crave to see.'

Lauri smiled at the idea of theatregoers craving to see her. She watched a gnat on the cup of a nearby flower,

combing its green wings with its legs. The careless dex-
terity reminded her of Andreya.

'Have you decided to present *Giselle* this coming
season, Max?' The Contessa smiled nostalgically. 'I
always love it, and recall how wonderful your dear
grandmother was in the role.'

'*Giselle* is a weakness I can never resist,' his smile
warmed his eyes brilliantly. 'Yes, I shall be presenting
the ballet at the Fenice when we open the new season.'

'With Andreya?' Venetia glanced sideways at him,
and it seemed to Lauri that her blue eyes held a flash
of dislike which she quickly veiled with her lashes.

'Andreya is my *prima ballerina*.' He gazed reflectively
into the glass in his hand. 'She came to me six years
ago and in that time my company has had some exciting
successes. Giselle is not one of her best roles, I will
admit –'

'Are you blindly loyal, Max? That woman is as hard
as nails!'

The words rang out in the loggia, and they all stared
at Venetia, whose flash of animation made her lovely.
Then she leapt to her feet, a hand pressed against her
mouth. 'Oh, Max, how could I say such a thing – I
must be going out of my mind!'

'My dear –'

'No, don't be kind to me, Max. Because I can't live
with myself there is no reason why I should hurt others
– you of all people. You came to me in Florence when
I needed a friend as never before. Without you standing
by, I should have –'

'Venetia, don't torture yourself.' He rose quickly and
put an arm around her, and as Lauri watched them
she felt her fast-beating heart.

'I think it is time we went into lunch.' The Contessa

shook the white cat out of her lap and indicated that Lauri give her an arm. Talking together about the scented shrubs and trees, they made their way indoors as though nothing had happened. Venetia and Maxim walked behind them, but what they said to each other was not audible.

They lunched in the *salotto,* and the Contessa talked vivaciously about ballet. After several cups of Italian coffee, she said it was time for her siesta and she would join them later. Venetia also excused herself, and after Maxim's perusal of a newspaper, he asked Lauri if she would like to see a little more of the island.

'We are informal here,' he added with a rather strained smile. 'I am a friend of such long standing that the villa is more or less a second home to me.'

Lauri felt the disquiet in him as they walked the cool length of the *salotto,* with its inlaid floor, wall murals and vases of flowers on pedestals. As they approached the archway into the garden, her glance was caught by the three crossed spears on the wall above the arch. 'In the days of Roman conquest, crossed spears were a symbol of subjugation,' Maxim smiled down at her with a hint of savagery as she looked at them. 'The slave of a Roman had to pass beneath them to indicate her bondage.'

'How interesting,' she said, trying to sound casual as she preceded him beneath the three symbolical spears.

'There are Roman ruins on the island,' he added, 'and a cave down on the shore where secret rites were practised long ago. Would you like to see it?'

'Very much.' The flagstones were hot, the walls of the villa very white, and she took her sunglasses out of her bag and put them on. Now she could look at him and she saw that he still had a faintly savage look . . . due, she was sure, to that scene in the loggia.

'I had better warn you that the rites were connected with Aphrodite, the goddess of love.' His teeth gleamed against his tawny skin. 'The islanders say that the cave is haunted by the pagan spirit of love, and that a woman alone there with a man is in danger of falling under Aphrodite's spell.'

'What of the man?' Lauri asked daringly. 'Doesn't the spell affect him as well?'

'I had better not tell you, especially after our conversation in the gondola coming here.'

His words and his mood were unsettling, and a tingle seemed to run along her spine as he followed her past the loggia where Venetia had cried out that he was blind about Andreya. The loggia looked like a house of flowers, with bees dark against the pink and white clematis, and the pulse-beat of the cicadas was echoed by Lauri's pulses as she hurried ahead of Maxim down the terrace steps.

'Be careful,' he warned her, 'you don't want a twisted ankle.'

Oh, heavens, she wanted to retort. Let me forget for once about my precious dancing feet!

The view beyond the terrace was lovely and limitless. The other islands were smudges of purple, and there was a haze fine as a bridal veil stretched across the horizon. The sea lipped the shore as she reached it, almost as green as jade. The sand was fine underfoot, and almost as black as ebony.

'I've never seen a black beach before.' No shadow fell across hers as Maxim joined her; his strides were always unhurried and lithe. She knelt down and was surprised to find the dark sand hot from the sun that it did not reflect. She trickled it through her fingers and over the whiteness of her arms. 'It's like crushed onyx and black pearls,' she laughed.

Maxim towered into the sun above her, and as she looked up at him she saw with surprise that he had discarded his jacket and his tie – somewhere up there on the terrace – and that his white shirt lay open at his throat.

So must his roving ancestors have looked, standing on the quarterdeck of a ship as it set sail for a voyage of discovery. Same black brows linked above eyes that never wavered, the Roman nose like a prow above the stern upper lip and the passionate lower one.

'Come.' He held out a hand and she let him pull her to her feet. She had a natural lightness that brought her a little too close to him, and her eyes widened with the sudden shock of his nearness, and her own awareness of how alone they were on this black beach with its cave of Aphrodite, its scent of wild myrtle, and the soft, seductive murmurs of the sea.

'You look alarmed,' he murmured. 'Are you afraid that I am going to carry out my threat of this morning?'

She heard the quick catch of her own breath, and then his hand was at the base of her neck, curving round it in lean strength. She struggled and tried to turn her face away as his lips drew near to hers. She had never been so afraid in her life, and she went rigid as she felt his breath stir warmly against her cheek.

'Don't use me as a means of working off your temper,' she gasped.

'What do you mean?' He forced her to look at him, and she saw the flicker of dark fire in his eyes and felt his fingers in her hair.

'Y-you've been in a nasty mood since before lunch,'

she said breathlessly. 'Because of what Venetia said to you – '

'And what did Venetia say?' His voice was low and silken.

'You know very well.' Lauri's voice was low and shaken.

His arms tightened about her, and she knew that her heart was beating its wildness against his. 'Please – stop devilling me,' she implored.

For a long moment his eyes looked dangerous, and she prayed that he would spare her his kiss of mockery, of curiosity, and punishment. 'Is that how you think of me, as a devil?' he asked whimsically.

'Yes – at the moment.' She was beyond choosing her words; all she wanted was to be free of his arms.

'Does that mean that you regret coming to Venice to dance for me?'

'Would you allow me to return to England?' she fenced.

'No, I don't start something and leave it unfinished,' and then with a taunting little laugh he brushed her cheek with his lips and put her away from him. 'I promised to show you the cave of Aphrodite – unless you feel that I am too much of a devil to be alone with in there.'

'Is that the cave?' She ran ahead of him towards some strangely shaped rocks at the entrance of a hollow in the cliffs. The rocks were dark, like petrified dragons put there to guard the pagan secrets of the cave; she scrambled past brambles and wild myrtle until she stood within the mouth of the cave.

She took off her sunglasses and when the brambles rustled behind her, took a step forward into the large chamber of rock. 'Magic was born in old caves.' Maxim stood gazing around him. 'In such places the old sibyls told fortunes and sold love potions to young girls.'

'Do you believe in magic, *signor*?' The light that filtered in was sea-green, and Lauri felt a draught blowing against her cheek like a cobweb. It cooled the hollow under her cheekbone, where his brief kiss lingered.

'I believe that people's lives are shaped by deep, mysterious currents,' he replied. 'But perhaps by magic you mean nymphs and little green men who cast spells and lead people into mischief?'

'I should imagine they do exist,' she said with a laugh, 'judging from the things we do get led into, quite against our better judgment.'

'You consider that it was against your better judgment to come to Venice with my company?' He faced her, lounging against a waist-high boulder at the centre of the cave which had the look of a pagan altar of sacrifice.

'Sometimes,' she admitted. 'I have left Aunt Pat all on her own – yes, I know she's ambitious for me, but I've never been all that ambitious for myself.'

'You feel that you are sacrificing yourself to the ambitions of other people?' He touched the altar-like boulder significantly. 'But don't you realize that a person with a talent must share it? That it is not a personal property but a public one?'

'Yes, I realize that,' she gave a sigh, 'but surely you are talking about the kind of talent which Andreya has? Which your own grandmother had?'

'And which you have,' he said quietly, deliberately, yet in a voice that disturbed the shadows all around them. 'I thought it intriguing when I first saw your likeness to Travilla, the wide, winged eyebrows, the luminous eyes, the intangible quality of a being from another world lost in this one. You danced like an amateur that first time, but I knew I could remedy that.'

'How egotistical you are,' she broke in. 'It is always what you want – '

'Yes, when it comes to the dance,' he admitted. 'I have decided that I want you to partner Lonza in *Giselle*, perhaps when we go to London and you are more used to being on a stage.'

'But Andreya would never agree to sharing the role,' Lauri gasped.

'I am afraid she will have to.' His eyes held Lauri's, darkly brilliant in the gloom of the cave. 'Giselle is a poignant and lovely role. It demands a compassionate heart, the innocence that makes her betrayal believable. Andreya is a dancer of many unique gifts, but she brings to the role of Giselle the hysteria of her own selfish unhappiness.'

'*Signor*,' the word broke from Lauri, 'how can you say such a thing when you feel as you do – '

'How do I feel – like a lover?' His words struck with mocking resonance against the walls of the cave. 'Good heavens, have we really given the impression that she has my heart, and I have hers?'

He was laughing, making echoes that mocked, and there was such a look of recklessness about him that Lauri backed away involuntarily from his hard, lean figure, and his laughter.

'The woman I love is on this island.' He spoke with a rampant frankness, and suddenly he began to pace the cave like a panther on a leash His white shirt took on green shadows, and his eyes glinted. 'I have loved her, it seems, for ever, but I must wait, be a little more patient, for something stands between us and she is not yet ready to love me.'

Love me . . . love me . . . the echoes of his words died away and all that remained was the knowledge that he spoke about Venetia. She was the woman he loved on this island set in opal water; this remote and pagan place that opened the heart and made it reveal its secrets.

Lauri looked about her with a cold little shiver, and wanted to be gone from this place. 'I understand,' she said, and it was the simple truth. She could understand his love for Venetia, but she had always thought it strange that he could care for Andreya.

'Come, it is cold in here after the warmth of the sun.' He took her arm in light fingers and as they emerged from the cave, it seemed to her that the mist on the horizon had crept a little nearer to the island.

'Are we leaving soon?' she asked.

'Zena will expect us to stay for dinner. Why,' he followed her gaze to the sea, 'are you afraid that the sea mist is creeping in to encircle us?'

'It does appear to be thickening,' she said. 'Surely it would cut this island off from the mainland?'

'From all civilization for several hours,' he said dryly. 'I have been here before when the mist has developed into a fog – but the beds at the villa are comfortable.'

'You mean we would have to remain here overnight?' Lauri's heart gave a flutter of dismay.

'It would be the wise thing to do,' he agreed.

'But surely it would be even wiser to leave before the mist develops?' Lauri tried to sound matter-of-fact. 'I am sure the Contessa would understand   '

'I don't wish to leave just yet.' His eyes held a wayward

glint as they met Lauri's. 'It is an exciting experience to be cut off from the world, almost like being lost in the clouds.'

And of course, Lauri added to herself as they walked to the edge of the sea, he would be near Venetia a few more hours. Green ripples touched the margin of the black sands, and not so far out the drifting mist made lace that could grow into a web that would hold them trapped.

'I suppose I must bow to the inevitable,' she said. 'I know by now that you don't yield once you have made up your mind.'

'You make me sound very self-willed,' he mocked.

'All men are that, you more than most,' she rejoined.

'Just listen to the voice of experience!' He laughed above her head. 'Like most females, Miss Garner, you are swayed by your emotions like the tide by the moon and cannot understand the logic which governs a man's actions.'

'It is hardly logical to think I am ready to dance the role of Giselle,' she argued. 'Andreya has had years of experience – and besides, she would never let another dancer have the role.'

'I am the Director of the di Corte Company,' now he spoke curtly. 'My dancers will do as I say.'

'But I couldn't – you and Michael are out of your minds to suggest it – '

'So Lonza has talked of wanting you for his partner?'

Her glance flashed upwards to meet Maxim's. 'You must have heard him say so, *signor,* when you passed us on the stairs yesterday.'

'Ah, so that was what he meant?' A black lock of Maxim's hair was teased by the sea breeze. 'I must say I wondered.'

'What else would he mean?' She looked at Maxim uncomprehendingly.

'If you don't know, my child, then it is proof indeed that innocence is its own defence.' His smile was the rare and brilliant one that had the power to disarm his enemies and enslave his dancers. As she looked at him her hair blew free like a swallowtail, and she wondered how long he had loved Venetia, and whether so proud and tempestuous a man could ever be content with half a woman's heart.

'You don't always like me, do you?' He smiled as if it didn't really worry him. 'Being older than you, *signorina*, I know that people never really come to terms with each other until they have dug below the surface of each other and caused a pain or two. It must hurt, the learning of another person. The faults have to be understood as well as the virtues admired, the talents applauded, and the physical attributes found attractive.

'That is life,' he added quietly. 'Life, as Victor Hugo wrote so wisely, is the flower of which love is the honey.'

She absorbed the quotation, along with the tang of the sea and the evasive scent of wild myrtle. Had she ever really believed that Maxim di Corte had a cold heart? Well, she had learned today on this Venetian island that she had been wrong.

They were making their way up the terrace steps when Lauri noticed that the strands of sea mist had formed into a mesh that obscured the sun. Threads of flame shot through the mesh, and as Lauri caught her breath at the sight, she stumbled on a step and fell flat before she could save herself. In an instant Maxim had lifted her to her feet. 'Have you hurt an ankle?' he demanded, when she winced.

'No, but just look at my stocking – and my skirt!'

The violet material had ripped about two inches, and her knee was grazed.

'You should be more careful,' Maxim said, an arm around her waist as she limped into the villa. 'You could so easily have wrenched an ankle.'

'Blow my ankles,' she retorted, 'it's my skirt I'm worried about. Just look at that tear!'

'What has happened?' Venetia rose from a deep window-seat of the *salottino* and came over to them.

'The child was not looking where she was going,' Maxim told her.

'I'm not a child,' Lauri muttered, dabbing at her grazed knee.

'That knee must be bathed,' Venetia said gently. 'Come, we will go up to my room and do what is necessary. Maxim, perhaps you will ring for some tea. Zena is probably awake by now, and she likes her afternoon cup of tea.'

'Certainly, my dear,' he said, and frowned at Lauri. 'I am sure Venetia can lend you a dress, for we are dining here, mist or no mist.'

'Max, don't be such a bully,' Venetia chided him. 'Do you want to make Laurina cry?'

'I am sure it would take more than my bullying to make *Laurina* cry.' He bore down deliberately on the Italianized name, and Lauri gave him a look meant to scorch but which left him looking cool. He bowed herself and Venetia from the room.

After seeing to Lauri's knee and applying a small plaster to the graze, Venetia took her along to the Italian Room, which she and her husband had shared whenever they stayed together at the villa. Some of her dresses from those lost and happy times were still hanging in the wardrobe, she added, and it was with an effort, Lauri saw, that she forced herself to turn the handle and push open the door of the big double room.

It was tapestried, with a baroque carved four-poster bed, massive closets, embroidered chairs, and big windows overlooking the sea. Venetia stood looking about her, sadness etching her face and shadowing her deep blue eyes. 'The remembrance of happiness is more painful than the recollection of torment,' she said. 'I look in those mirrors and see Stefano's face, not my own. I touch this bedside clock and time has no more meaning for me, for it cannot bring him back in an hour, in two hours. It ticks away my empty life.'

'Venetia,' Lauri touched her arm with gentle fingers, 'I am sure that one day your life will be full again, happy again.'

'There is no happiness like that which comes from being loved and needed,' Venetia said, and as she reached forward to open the doors of a wardrobe her tapering hands seemed to be reaching for what was gone. A mixture of materials shimmered within the wardrobe, and after a moment Venetia drew out a simply styled dress of luscious green-gold material. 'I am sure this will fit you.' She held it up against Lauri. 'Yes, we are of a similar build.'

'It's very lovely.' Lauri fingered the brocade, and then added from her impulsive heart : 'I am sure you are needed, Venetia, and loved.'

'Perhaps.' Venetia shrugged and laid the green-gold dress across the foot of the baroque bed. 'I will leave the dress here for you to change into later. You will not mind using this room? It has its ghosts, but they are young and very much in love, and they cannot hurt anyone but me.'

Lauri's throat tightened with compassion, then she

followed Venetia from the Italian Room. She would not be afraid to return to it, she told herself.

Later, as she stood in the brocade dress before the dressing-table mirror and fixed her hair in a braid about her head, she remembered Venetia's words and her own childish sense of irrevocable loss years ago. Aunt Pat had taken her into warm arms and had not needed words to convey what had happened to her adored parents — they were gone and all she had left was the memory of their gaiety, their beauty, their love for her.

She loved Aunt Pat deeply and warmly, but there had often been nights when she had wept for the special smile that had been her mother's, and the hard hug and smoky kiss that had been her father's.

It might be years before Venetia was ready to love again, and able to let her little son be reborn out of the new love.

Lauri drew a sigh, and went to look out of the windows of the Italian Room. Her sigh turned to a gasp of dismay — with the falling of darkness a thick curtain of mist had drawn round the island, isolating it from the rest of the world.

She could hear phantom bells drifting over the water — the bells of Venice guiding the ships into harbour. The quickening beat of her heart told her that the Villa Nora had become a 'castle of no return'.

She listened to the bells and the beat of her heart, and suddenly the shadows beyond the dressing-table lamps had drawn closer to her and the room felt haunted. She turned, snatched up her long skirts and fled from the room and along the corridor to the stairs. There was an archway just before she reached them, and a sound of voices brought her up short, and she stood like a girl in a medieval frame, the brocade dress shimmering green-gold about her slight figure.

Then Venetia spoke, and there wasn't time for Lauri to advance or retreat. She heard the young widow say clearly : 'I know your feelings, Maxim. I have loved too deeply myself not to sense an equally deep emotion in someone else.'

'I thought you might guess how things stood with me, *cara*.' His voice was that of a man very much moved. 'I shall wait, and hope that soon my love will be returned as I need it. I cannot accept mere affection, or any of the lesser forms of love. You understand that, Venetia ?'

'Utterly,' she replied. 'For you, Max, all or nothing.'

Lauri trembled. Her heart beat fast, for it was as though she had pressed the spring of a secret drawer and found within something she had not wanted to face. She moved, and Maxim must have heard the rustle of her dress. He swung to face her, and his eyes were shadowed by his black brows.

'Ah, there you are.' He studied her in the lovely borrowed dress, and added with a brief smile : 'I have never seen you look so grown up.'

'Thank you,' she said, and walked quietly down the stairs between him and Venetia.

Candles were alight in the Venetian chandeliers of the *salotto*. A fire had been lit, and the long curtains were drawn against the mist and the phantom bells. The scene was cosy and warm, but Lauri's heart felt strangely chilled.

CHAPTER NINE

A WEEK had gone by since Lauri had stayed for a mist-bound night at the Villa Nora. Rehearsals for the new ballet season had begun in earnest, and Maxim had announced that Lauri was understudying Andreya in the role of Giselle.

Lauri still shivered when she remembered Andreya's face. A buzz went round among the other dancers and significant glances were exchanged. 'Watch out,' Lauri was warned. 'Andreya brooks no rivals for a role.'

'I don't want the role,' Lauri said. 'The very thought of it frightens the wits out of me.'

This was true. She was sure she would run away if Maxim gave in to his impulse to see her in the ballet. It would be cruel of him, for he knew her secret fears as no one else in the company knew them, and he knew also that her youth and sensitivity, her likeness to Travilla, were not real substitutes for experience and technical brilliance.

Maxim, she assured herself, would not run the risk of a failure just for the sake of a whim.

She said as much to Michael as they stood on the Rialto watching the sun sink into the Grand Canal. He fired a cigarette, dropped the match into the darkening water, and puffed a plume of smoke. 'What if Andreya breaks a leg?' he chuckled. 'You mystify me, Lauri. Love of the dance consumes the rest of us, but what is it that you love?'

'Does one have to be consumed by the things one loves?' she asked.

'Yes.' His cigarette smoke drifted into the purple twilight. 'It is a law of nature, for the world of the emotions is a jungle. You know, Lauri, if you are not careful you will find yourself desperately in love with a man, a much more dangerous undertaking than being a lover of the dance.'

She met his glance, which held challenge and curiosity. A pulse in her throat gave a quick little beat. 'What are you, Lauri?' he murmured. 'An elusive sorceress, or an unawakened child?'

'I am neither,' she said, with her husky laugh. 'I am just an ordinary English girl caught up with a lot of brilliant people who say the oddest things. Aunt Pat will love hearing about all of you when, as I hope, she comes here for the start of the ballet season. I've written to ask her,' Lauri clasped her hands together on the parapet of the bridge, 'and I do hope she'll be well enough to make the journey. It would make such a difference, having her with me. I should feel much more confident.'

'Any wish of yours is my wish, too,' Michael said in his foreign way that was so disarming at times. The waters of Venice flowed under the centuries-old bridge, and from an open-air restaurant drifted the Tales from the Vienna Woods, lovely and lilting. 'Shall we dance?' Michael hummed a snatch of the music.

'Ballet dancers waltz badly,' she said, peering over the bridge at the water that was becoming star-sprinkled.

'Are you looking for mermaids?' She felt Michael's arm slide round her waist. 'There, lean a little forward – do you see that one with the long dark hair, the white skin and mysterious eyes? She uses the dance to lure her victims to her.'

'You fool!' Lauri laughed, and at once with a strong,

dexterous movement of his arm he swung her close to him and pitched his cigarette into the water.

'You owe me a tribute, you little devil, and now you'll pay it.' Her protest was smudged from her lips by his, and to anyone passing by in a gondola or on the banks of the canal, they were sweethearts kissing on the Rialto.

The girl was seen to struggle, and a gondolier called out to another one, 'What of it? Love without a little fighting is like potatoes without salt.'

Lauri heard the laughter as the boats sped beneath the bridge, and breaking free of Michael she ran, off the bridge, under an arcade, and down an alleyway. She hurried on under the lamps that cast sudden pools of light that made the shadows seem denser, uncaring that she might lose herself in this Venetian maze of alleys. Her feelings were in a tumult. All she could think of was that things would be better when Aunt Pat came.

Dear Aunt Pat, she must come. She was the only refuge Lauri was sure of.

The next day came, and the next, and no letter arrived from England. But Lauri discovered that rehearsal time was so busy, so filled with urgency, that there was little time left for any personal brooding. The striving, creative tension, the aching muscles, the sounds of music heard all over the *palazzo*, helped to dispel a fugitive depression.

The great mirrors of the hall reflected the leaping imp-cats, the linked cygnets, the enraptured maenads. Bruno's arm sliced the air as he counted, while his assistant thrummed the piano.

Maxim was like dark lightning at the centre of the storm, being consulted on the music, the décor, the costumes. There was nothing he did not know about the mood and content of each ballet, and apart from that he was arranging the publicity and the design of the posters and programmes. There were daily cables and calls from the European capitals the company would tour when the opening of the new season had been started in Venice.

Piano scores and stage sketches littered tables and chairs, and while the beat of the dance echoed through the *palazzo*, discussions went on with artists, wardrobe staff and musicians. Victor Arquest, the composer and conductor, was at the *palazzo* night and day, a fiery friend of Maxim's who understood the art of ballet music as Stravinsky had understood it.

He played the piano like a wicked angel, and at the end of a long, strenuous day it felt good to relax in chairs and listen to the music, and talk. How they talked! They discussed each ballet in detail, for they were all part of what was being created. The *feu sacré* burned in each one of them, and Vitya, as they called the composer, would call for more coffee, and silence, for he had another inspiration. The music resounded, up to the painted ceiling, and the world of reality went on outside while these egotists, these wild and lovely people, created their own special magic which in three short weeks would be presented to the world.

Every detail, every movement from the little to the large was being brought to life and any day now they would go by steamer to the Fenice for their first stage rehearsal.

Lauri felt apprehensive, and was glad of the urgency of the hours through which she now lived. Michael was kept as busy as she, and there was no time, no place, for them to be alone. Sometimes their eyes would meet across a crowded room, and her heart that had grown up told her that he wanted only a love affair with her. The entire meaning of life lay for him in his dancing career. His work possessed him and his heart.

It was the best and only life for him, a complete dedication. For her the future loomed like a chasm which she must leap alone – all she could hope for was that Aunt Pat would be waiting in the wings of the Fenice the night she danced in a theatre for the first time.

But still there was no letter from her, and the hours were rushing by, taking with them the days and nights. Lauri rushed off early to the post-office, the day they were to go to the Fenice for the first time, and sent off a telegraph wire to her aunt. 'Are you quite well?' she wired. 'Please let me know. I love you and need you, if you can come.'

She came out of the post-office in a worried trance, and when she reached the small bridge that crossed to the *palazzo*, Maxim was waiting, tall, dark and rather grim on the other side. 'Where have you been?' he asked.

She told him, and saw his lips tighten. 'My aunt is more important to me than your ballet rehearsal,' she flared.

'I realize that, child – '

'I'm sure you don't.' She brushed past him and went to join members of the *corps de ballet*, who chattered like jays on the landing stage, holding in their hands the square cases that held practice clothes, a bottle of *eau de cologne*, and a rough Turkish towel for a rub down after rehearsal. Apples too, probably, and maybe an orange or banana. Each dancer guarded zealously her wand-like figure and smooth complexion, and Lauri thought often that Maxim di Corte had one of the best-

looking dancing companies, as well as one of the most
disciplined.

'I put your things in with mine.' Concha gazed at her
English friend with concern in her Latin eyes. 'You are
very troubled, is this not so, *chiquita*?'

'Yes.' Lauri bit her lip, and gazed at the shimmer of
the canal water and the green reflections from sea-mould
on stone. She told herself fiercely that Maxim couldn't
keep her here if Aunt Pat was sick. He hadn't that
power, to keep her away from the one person who really
cared about her.

'Perhaps your Tia Pat plans a lovely surprise for you
and is already on her way to Venice.' Concha's eyes
flashed eagerly, 'Yes, it is very possible, Lauri. You
British people, after all, are very unpredictable.'

'No more than most,' Lauri said, but her eyes had
brightened. It would be like Aunt Pat to spring such a
lovely surprise on her, and she had her fingers crossed
as with the other dancers she climbed into the steamer
that was to take them to the Fenice Theatre.

The front of the Fenice was impressive and columned,
and the auditorium inside was almost circular. There
were tiers of handsome boxes, and above the stage the
carved, mythical phoenix that gave the theatre its name.

The dancers changed into their leotards in the rather
chilly dressing-rooms at the rear of the stage. Lauri felt
cold with nerves, taut as a violin string, and she was
relieved when the cast of *The Firebird* were called on-
stage.

Concha was dancing the role of the Firebird, and she
tossed a scarlet shawl to Lauri as she ran past her.
Lauri drew it around her, over her black leotard, as she
stood in the wings watching the vivacious Latin girl
dancing across the boards to the spot where the golden

apple tree would stand. She was pursued by the princely hero, while an eerie spotlight was played over the Petrified Knights, sweethearts of the princesses abducted by the sinister magician into whose castle garden the Firebird had flown.

Maxim was directing from the left of the stage, a black sweater to his chin, his black hair as tousled as that of his dancers. Lauri looked at him, and electricity seemed to curl about her heart. His eyes were leaping like the 'devils' on-stage. He looked utterly determined that each member of his company should give body, heart and spirit to the forthcoming season.

The proceeds of the first night in Venice were to go towards the restoration of farms and homes destroyed in the floods that had swept through Italy last year, and Lauri knew suddenly that she would not be able to walk out on a ballet company so dedicated. She closed her eyes there in the wings of the theatre and prayed that Concha was right and that Aunt Pat was on her way to Venice already.

When Lauri opened her eyes, she felt the force of a strange silence behind her. She turned round and found herself face to face with Lydia Andreya. Lauri tensed. Her hand touched her mouth as though to stop a small cry of alarm. She stood like a helplessly magnetized moth – with flame close to her wings.

'What are you afraid of?' Andreya's smile was mocking, and her hair was drawn back from her strange eyes in a *calot* of gold. 'I have no need to harm you, you will do that yourself when you go out on to that stage. You are afraid of it, eh? Afraid of its rake, the rows of seats below, the proscenium arch above, and the phoenix in flames – '

'*Don't!*' Lauri backed from the ballerina, almost to

the edge of the stage where it sloped to the orchestra pit. The fall behind her was dark and deep, and she and Andreya were curiously isolated from the rest of the company. Someone was playing the *Firebird* music at the piano, dancers were skimming and leaping across stage, while Maxim was now in discussion with the couple who had designed the settings for the new ballets, a voluble French husband and wife who were both arguing at the same time.

Lauri could hear the nasal French voices, the deep pitch of Maxim's, the beat of the music and her own heart. Andreya drew a step nearer to her, and again she backed away. The scarlet shawl quivered against her black leotard like flame. . . .

'You know you will make a fool of yourself out on that stage,' Andreya taunted. 'Everyone will laugh at you – *I* am the dancer that people pay money to come and see. Without me the di Corte Company would be nothing – nothing do you hear?'

Lauri heard, but Andreya's voice was pitched low so that no one else could do so. Nearby a stage-hand was hammering, his back turned to them. Andreya's mouth was the line of a bow drawn taut to aim her poisoned arrows.

'What have you got that anyone would pay money to see?' Her eyes swept Lauri from head to toe. 'No beauty, no brilliance, only your false air of innocence. Men are always fooled by that sort of thing, and everyone here has seen you using it on Lonza – and on Maxim.'

'That isn't true,' Lauri gasped.

'I must say,' Andreya laughed softly, 'that you put on a very good act of injured innocence. Is that how you got Maxim to promise you the role of Giselle?'

'Maxim has done no such thing.' Lauri could feel a

tremor rising from the backs of her knees and running all through her body. 'I am merely your understudy, and quite safe in that respect from ever having to dance the role.'

'You think so?' Andreya arched her eyebrows. 'What if I were deliberately sick the first night of the new season, just for the fun of seeing you laughed off this stage? There is nothing crueller than the scorn of an audience – unless it is the panic of one. Panic,' Andreya spoke softly and drew another step nearer to Lauri, 'fear of fire, screams as a defective boiler explodes and the stage is curtained by flames. . . .'

As in a nightmare, Lauri was a child again, running from her bed to the boarding-house window that faced the theatre where her parents were dancing. A loud noise had woken her, and when with shaking young hands she pulled aside the curtains, she saw people and flames shooting from the theatre. The dome above it, that made it look like a temple, was tongued by flames. People were rushing into the road and screaming. There was a clang of firebells . . . a toll of doom in young Lauri's heart. . . .

As she swayed, there on the brink of the orchestra pit, hands caught at her. She was lifted and held and carried to a dressing-room. Someone gave her some brandy and after that she felt a little better.

'Go home with her to the *palazzo*.' There was anger in the deep voice, and Lauri glanced up and saw Maxim standing behind Viola, who was holding her hands and chafing them. His face was as angry as his voice, and Lauri felt cold and wished she could say that she felt all right and could go on with her part in the rehearsal.

But she couldn't say it. She wanted, desperately, to get out of the haunting atmosphere of the theatre, with its musky scent of greasepaint that reminded her of a day long ago, when she had sat on her father's knee in front of a dressing-room mirror and he had run a fat stick of greasepaint round her childish face. 'It's in your blood, Lauri baby,' her father had laughed gaily. 'You will no more escape it than we ever could.'

He had smiled into the mirror at her mother, and Lauri had felt safe and secure in their love for her and each other.

'Viola,' she spoke quietly, 'you don't have to come with me.'

'You will do as I say.' Maxim frowned as he spoke, and Lauri wanted to say that she didn't need a keeper. She wouldn't run away, because no matter how far you ran you couldn't escape from yourself.

'Signor di Corte,' she met his eyes, darker than ever because of the drawn-down visor of his black eyebrows, 'I shall be all right, and I don't wish to upset your rehearsal more than necessary. Please let Viola stay. She loves to dance so much.'

'Very well.' He gave Viola a brief smile. 'Go back on-stage, little one.'

The pretty Italian dancer smiled and padded off in her ballet slippers. Lauri heard Maxim sigh, and wondered why he bothered with someone as complicated as herself. 'I'm sorry,' she said. 'For upsetting things – '

'Things are certainly upset.' He prowled up and down the dressing-room. 'I have put up with a lot from Andreya, but not this. This intimidation of another dancer I will not tolerate. She goes – '

'Signor,' Lauri jumped to her feet, 'let me go, then things will settle down. Andreya is too valuable to you – '

'Valuable?' He stood still, like a great, dark graceful

cat who had come to the end of his tether. 'Because I am just the master, eh, and my dancers mere puppets? Because in your estimation I place dancing ability above humanity, compassion, love for others?'

'That's business, isn't it?' Lauri said tiredly.

'Yes, just business.' There was a flare to his nostrils, and the black sweater seemed to cast shadow in his chin cleft. 'I am glad you realize it, for tomorrow you will start rehearsing *Giselle* with Lonza.'

As Lauri stood looking at him, stunned and dismayed, he swung towards the door of the dressing-room. 'Andreya has been threatening for some time to leave this company,' he threw over his shoulder. 'She has had big offers from her own country to go there and dance as a star, so you need not worry that you are the cause of the rift between her and me.'

'But she depends on you,' Lauri said helplessly.

'Andreya depends on no one,' he rejoined. 'Only those with a heart have such a need, poor fools.'

He strode off down the passage that led to the stage, and Lauri was left alone. There were nylon tights thrown over a screen, a box spilling ribbons, and a little glass of brandy dregs on the dressing-table. The sound of the piano drifted along the passage outside, and the scent of greasepaint was pervasive.

Lauri's knees shook and she sat down again as the full force of Maxim's decision hit her.

Here at the theatre of the phoenix – the bird in flames – she must dance the role of Giselle. She must remember everything Maxim had taught her about the ballet. Every subtle gesture, every nuance, every step. She must forget, if she could, every taunting word of Andreya's.

She dressed in a while, and made her way out of the theatre by a side door. She walked about aimlessly, looking at things in the shops, and trying to feel the reality of what that scene with Andreya had led to. She found herself in front of the Madonna Café and went in for a cup of coffee. From the window beside her table she could see the Fenice, so romantically old and columned, where Travilla had danced long ago.

The crowds had loved her, but what would be their reaction to the Giselle her grandson would spring on them in two weeks' time?

Lauri drank her coffee in an attempt to find warmth, but when she rose to leave the café she had made a decision. She returned to the theatre and stayed for the remainder of the rehearsal. Maxim made no comment, but she thought she saw a gleam of approval in his eyes

Two mornings later Lauri received an answer to the wire she had sent to Aunt Pat. It came in the form of a letter from their neighbour at Downhollow – who was writing for Aunt Pat because her arthritis was affecting her hands and making it awkward for her to write personally to her niece. She had also delayed writing because she had hoped very much to be able to make the journey to Venice, but her doctor advised against it.

'I don't want you to worry about me,' ran the dictated letter. 'Concentrate on your dancing, Lauri, and on having a big success when you appear at the Fenice, which I am sure is a beautiful theatre. Signor di Corte has been kind enough to write to me, and he assures me you are doing well, and he has high hopes of you. He is a much kinder man, my dear, than I think you realize. I know you would like me with you at the present time, and I wish with all my heart that it were possible, but I am sure you can depend on Signor

Corte as much as on me. My arthritis is a nuisance, but you will be home in no time at all, and I shall be able to see you dance in London. I think of you constantly, Lauri dear, and send you all my love, all my best wishes, and all the strength I can. Dance for me, dear, and dance as I know you can.

Your most loving, and hopeful Aunt Pat.'

Tears smarted in Lauri's eyes when she came to the end of the letter. Poor Aunt Pat, having to put up with all that pain, and yet not complaining. Lauri read again the part in which her aunt said that Maxim had written to her. It was a thoughtful gesture, and made Lauri feel ashamed of the way she had behaved when he had said he understood her anxiety.

Venetia had also called him kind, and had seemed almost shocked that Lauri should consider him otherwise.

Lauri smiled wryly and wondered what Venetia and her aunt would say of the demon who conducted the rehearsals at the Fenice. She and the rest of the company had just returned from the theatre, where they had been dancing since early that morning, and Lauri had sought the privacy of the walled garden in order to read her letter.

She sighed as she folded it and put it in the pocket of her jacket. The backs of her legs ached and her toes felt a trifle sore, but the water-tinged breeze through the willows was comforting, and she leaned back in the garden seat and tried to relax. The water whispered beyond the old grey walls, and the bells of a nearby church made deep bronze music.

Had Maxim guessed that her toes felt sore? She had noticed his frown when she had made a mess of that series of lifts with Michael, before the final pose, sitting on his knee. It was difficult but so beautiful when performed correctly . . . oh lord, it wouldn't do for anything to go wrong with her toes.

Vines rustled as the sun died and dusk began to creep into the walled garden. She ought to be going in, but it was so peaceful here, a retreat from the constant talk about the new ballet season and the part she was to play in it. Everyone was amazingly helpful and encouraging, but at the back of the general kindness Lauri detected shades of doubt.

'Don't worry, everything will be fine,' they said to her, but dancers have speaking eyes, and Lauri knew that they were as worried as she was.

At rehearsal that afternoon she had felt the tension in the air when she had done those lifts so clumsily with Michael. Now added to her sore toes was the ache of disappointment that Aunt Pat would not be coming to Venice. . . .

Again the vines rustled, a bird twittered, and her spine stiffened as she heard footfalls. They were unhurried on the path leading to her retreat, and then a lean hand parted the veiling willow leaves and Lauri was discovered by Maxim.

He stood looking down at her, and the dusk merged with his eyes and shadowed their expression. 'I saw a letter awaiting you on the hall table,' he said. 'I guessed it was from your aunt – is she all right?'

'Her arthritis is very bad.' Lauri couldn't keep the concern out of her voice; nor the keen disappointment which the letter had brought her. 'She won't be able to be with me when the season opens.'

'I am sorry, I realize how much you were looking forward to her support.' He drew in his breath rather sharply. 'Now, of course, you feel that you must face everything on your own. *Le Sacre* – the virgin chosen for the sacrifice.'

'If you mean to be humorous,' she said shakily, 'I'm afraid I am not in a laughing mood.'

'No,' he agreed, 'something has been wrong with you all day.'

'I'm tired.' She jumped to her feet in sudden alarm. 'It's the nervous tension – '

'Come with me.' He caught hold of her hand and held it firmly in his. 'I want to have a look at those feet of yours.'

'M-my feet are all right.' She held back from him, but his fingers were like steel, hers like mere pins. She was drawn by him through the garden to his tower, and propelled up the spiral staircase ahead of him. The lamps were cosily alight in his tower room, and a manservant was laying the table.

For two, Lauri saw.

Maxim gestured at the sofa and she sat down, knowing it was useless to fight him. 'Off with your shoes and stockings,' he said. 'Come, there is no need for false modesty – I have seen legs before.'

Cheeks pink, eyes stormy, she turned aside from him and removed her flat-heeled shoes and seamless nylons. She felt like a child as with calm impersonality he took first her right foot in his hand, then her left one, and examined her toes. His fingers were lean and hard against her Achilles tendon, the most vulnerable part of a dancer's foot, and at last he glanced up at her.

'I suppose you would have gone on dancing with sore toes until you were unfit to dance at all,' he said curtly. 'The slippers you wear are not hand-made, I take it?'

She shook her head. 'Ballet slippers wear out so

quickly, and the ready-made sort are less expensive.'

'They are dearer in the long run, if a dancer has sensitive feet.' He turned to his manservant and said something in Italian. The man went out of the room, and returned with a jar of salve. Maxim handed it to Lauri and told her to rub some of it into her feet. 'Yes, right now,' he added, 'and before you go to bed. To-morrow I will take you to be fitted for new slippers, and you will promise me never to wear any other sort. Your feet are valuable to you, and vulnerable because they are still such young feet.'

'It's kind of you to worry about my feet.' She stressed the last two words as she applied the cool salve to her sore toes.

'You don't really think I am being kind.' She heard a glass stopper clink as he withdrew it from a decanter. 'You think I am safeguarding an investment.'

'Aren't you, *signor?*' She flexed her toes and had to admit to herself that they felt easier.

'Please rest my investment on this.' He slid a hassock towards her feet, and there was a smile of irony in his dark eyes as he handed her a glass of sherry. 'I happen to know that Michael Lonza is dining out tonight with some people who patronize the arts, so you are free to have dinner here with me.'

She glanced at the table and saw the candles in Venetian glass holders, and the flowers. 'I – I thought you were expecting someone special,' she said confusedly. 'I'm still in my everyday clothes – '

'Don't let that worry you.' His eyes flicked the bandeau that held back her hair, her face that was innocent of powder, and finally her small bare feet on the hassock. He was himself wearing a black velvet smoking jacket over immaculate grey trousers.

'Drink your sherry and relax,' he said lazily. 'Perhaps a little music will help.'

He went over to the stereo and put on a record. The music of *Swan Lake* drifted to Lauri, bringing back vividly to her mind her first encounter with Maxim di Corte. She had thought him the most intimidating man she had ever seen, with his proud Venetian face, his penetrating eyes, and infrequent smile.

She looked at him over the rim of her sherry glass and wondered if he was reading her mind. 'You took on quite a task, *signor*, when you decided to turn a duckling into a swan,' she smiled diffidently.

'I enjoy a challenge,' he leaned against the baluster of the small spiral staircase that led up to his book gallery, 'but if you had danced like a pudding I should still have taken you as a pupil.'

'Because I look a little like Travilla.' Lauri studied the portrait and saw the air of defencelessness about Travilla, the blend of poetry and wistful passion about her features, the brown eyes with motes of light in them. 'It's strange,' Lauri murmured, 'like looking into a pool and seeing one's reflection a little out of focus.'

'When you wear her costume to dance in *Giselle*, the audience at the Fenice will think they are seeing a ghost.'

Lauri cast a wide-eyed glance at Maxim. He inclined his head and smiled quietly. 'Yes, the costume she wears in the portrait. Even the headdress of leaves and flowers. They will help you, eh, to feel a little less alone?'

He swung away from her when he said that, and informed his manservant that he could bring in their first dish. Lauri slipped into her shoes and out of her jacket and went into the bathroom to wash her hands before joining Maxim at the table. He had lit the candles and turned out the lamps. The smell of the flowers seemed to grow stronger; dark crimson, hothouse roses, as sensuous as their perfume.

'What lovely flowers.' Lauri wondered again if he had been expecting someone special – Venetia perhaps – who had been unable at the last moment to come and dine with him. Lauri studied him through the screen of her lashes and glimpsed a look of tension about his lips; a smouldering in his eyes as he cast a glance at the roses she had just admired. Was he thinking that they were wasted on her?

'Roses are like women,' he said. 'They change with the hours, and are lovelier by candlelight than in the glare of sunshine.'

He poured their wine into the Venetian goblets Lauri remembered from that other unexpected meal with him in his tower. She glanced round the circular room with its gleam of old polished wood, its books, and Travilla's woodland eyes upon them. Everything about the room was designed for repose, yet Lauri was aware of a play of tension, as definite as the flutter of the candle flames between herself and Maxim.

Delectable pieces of fish in a wine sauce were placed in front of her. 'To the recovery of your aunt's good health.' Maxim raised his wine glass. 'I am sure she will be with you in spirit if not in actuality, when you dance next week at the Fenice.'

Lauri's heart skipped a beat. 'Next week?' she echoed, and took a quick gulp of wine for courage.

'Will it be so bad for you, because your aunt will not be coming to Venice?' Maxim captured her eyes across the roses and the candle flames. 'You will have Lonza for a partner, and I shall be standing by. I shall be in the wings all the time.'

'Like my Svengali,' she smiled shakily.

'No,' he spoke with sudden harshness. 'I have never beguiled you into doing anything. I have only tried to bring out what is already in you. You foolish child, don't you understand yet?'

'I understood a long time ago,' she said, slightly unnerved by his sudden anger.

'What do you mean?' He stared across at her. 'What do you understand?'

'That you have always wanted to give to ballet-lovers another Travilla.' Lauri glanced down at her plate. 'I hope, *signor*, that I live up to your hopes of me.'

He sat silent, and in the end she looked at him. He was holding his wine glass in his long fingers, and the strangest smile was playing around his lips.

'You will make me a promise,' he said, 'always to stay as unworldly as you are now.'

'It seems a fairly easy promise to make.' She smiled and touched a fallen rose petal with her fingertip. 'The duckling will not turn easily into a swan, *signor*.'

'Talking of swans,' that slow smile of his grew into a flash of warmth, 'Lorenzo is going to give us one to eat.'

'I don't believe you,' Lauri gasped. 'How awful!'

'You had better not say that to Lorenzo,' Maxim laughed. 'He is quite proud of the bird, which is all white with a strawberry beak. He promises that it will be delectable.'

'I shan't eat a bite,' said Lauri, and she gave Lorenzo a most dubious look when he brought in the roast, with potatoes and other vegetables baked in the gravy.

Maxim sat laughing as though at a secret joke, then he said something to his manservant in Italian. Lorenzo beamed at Lauri as he set her plate in front of her, then he hurried away, and returned with a swan made

of vanilla and strawberry ice-cream, resting on a lake
of grape jelly.

'Lorenzo made it especially for you,' Maxim said.

'For me?' Lauri looked at him, then at Lorenzo, and
finally at the dark crimson roses. She seemed for a
moment to drown in their scent, then she came back
to reality with a little gasp. 'It's a lovely swan, Lorenzo,'
she smiled. 'It seems such a pity to eat it.'

'It would be a greater pity to let it melt away,' said
Maxim. 'You can't hold on to a rainbow, a bar of
music, or an ice-cream swan, my child. As you grow
older you will learn to love and let go.'

She met his eyes as Lorenzo went discreetly from the
room, carrying the swan back to the fridge for another
quarter of an hour. 'You can do that, *signor*?' Lauri
asked. 'Love – and let go?'

'If I have to,' he said, with a hint of gravity. 'You
cannot snatch at happiness, for it is like trying to take
hold of water, or a ray of sunlight. It just slips through
your fingers . . . now let us eat our veal before it gets cold.'

Lauri bent her head to her plate and ate obediently.
Although she could no longer see Maxim's eyes, their
expression of a moment ago remained with her. I can
love, and let go, he had said. Did that mean that he
knew Venetia might not be able to let go of her
memories so she would be free to love again?

'This veal is delicious – a little more wine, Laurina?'
Maxim smiled across at her enquiringly.

'No, I still have half a glass, *signor*.'

'Well, drink it up, it will do you good.'

'Yes, she said, and again she obeyed him. Laurina, he
had called her. Venetia's name for her.

They shared the vanilla and strawberry swan, and
afterwards they listened to a record of romantic piano

sonatas. Then Maxim said it was time for her to go to bed, and he escorted her to the hall of the *palazzo*. As he opened the door, a draught touched Lauri and she shivered. It was like the ghostly brush of fingers, and she drew back involuntarily against Maxim.

'What is the matter?' His breath stirred her hair.

'Oh,' she gave a nervous little laugh, 'I sometimes wonder if the *palazzo* is haunted.'

'All old houses have their ghosts.' He turned her towards him and studied her pale, triangular face in the shadowy light of the wall lamps. 'How odd we human beings are, how superstitious, and vulnerable,' he murmured. 'A mouse stirs in the shadows and we think we hear a footfall. A draught whispers along a stone floor and we think it is the silken skirts of a medieval lady. I have heard these little sounds myself, child. They are part of this old palace on the water, and I am sure you know really that your young imagination plays tricks with you.'

'Of course.' She drew away from him until his fingers alone held her by the wrists. '*Buona notte, signor.*'

'*Buona notte, signorina.*' He carried her wrists to his lips and kissed each one. 'You will not go to rehearsal tomorrow because I wish to have you fitted for new slippers. You have the salve for your feet?'

'In my pocket.' She smiled a little, and thought it typical of him to kiss her wrists, and discuss her feet almost in the same breath – her precious dancing feet. 'Thank you for the salve. My feet feel easier already.'

'I am glad to hear it – now off with you to your bed.'

As she slipped through the hall door, she turned a moment to glance at him. He stood tall and dark at the foot of his tower, and it might have been a trick of the shadows that made him look so lonely.

CHAPTER TEN

THIS was *the night*. Behind the scenes there was a lot of bustling about, excitement and tension, men moving scenery, women hurrying by with glittering costumes.

Out front the rows of seats and boxes were filling up with people clad for a gala performance. The attendants were periwigged and wearing gold-embroidered uniforms, there was a rustle of silk, the glitter of gems, and that intangible feeling of magic in the air which ballet creates for all those who love the art.

Everyone knew that a fresh young ballerina was dancing *Giselle* in place of Lydia Andreya, and curiosity was added to the general excitement. The girl was English, and very young. She had never danced a major role in public before . . . there was a rumour that she had been given the chance because she looked like Travilla di Corte.

'The girl may look like her,' said those who remembered Travilla, 'but no one these days has quite the enchanted quality that she had.'

Backstage, Lauri knew with every nerve what everyone must be thinking and saying. White with nerves, she added the eyelines that made her dusky-gold eyes look larger than ever. The bare electric light bulbs round the mirror showed her every contour of her face and her long, slim neck. Tonight her neck would be bowed under the sword of acclaim . . . or the sharp knife of criticism.

She was afraid, and so alone, for Maxim had allotted her a small dressing-room right at the end of the passage, away from the bustle of the other dancers. 'You will need to be tranquil before going on,' he had said. 'My other dancers are accustomed to first nights and they react to them as they would to a glass of wine. You are different.'

He had not elaborated on that remark, but Lauri had guessed what he meant. He could rely on his other dancers to the last pirouette . . . when she went out on to the stage of the Fenice it would rest with the gods whether she danced brilliantly or badly.

She touched the tiny leaves and flowers of the head-dress which Travilla had worn the last time she had danced in *Giselle*, and gave a little shiver as through the mirror she glimpsed the shrouded second act costume which a dresser would help her to put on. It looked ghostly in its white wrapper . . . the dress of a ghost who must surely be haunting this theatre tonight.

At that moment the dressing-room door was tapped upon. 'Come in!' Lauri called out. The door opened and there was a burst of colour and perfume as a smiling boy brought in a big basket of bird-of-paradise flowers, and a bouquet of myrtle, small lilies, and half a dozen golden rosebuds.

'How lovely!' Lauri ran to smell them, to touch them, and read the cards that were attached. The basket of flowers was from the members of the *corps de ballet*, who wished her luck on this her most important night.

Quick tears came to her eyes, and blurred the words on the other card.

'Lilies for innocence, golden rosebuds for youth, and myrtle – a token of the love we will dance for everyone tonight.'

Her heart gave a tiny jolt. The card was unsigned,

but she guessed at once that the sender of the bouquet and the note was Michael Lonza.

Michael, in whom was mingled all the fire and spirit of the dance. To whom love was an ecstasy of the body alone.

She touched the sprigs of myrtle and its scent wafted her to an island in the sun; she heard again the whisper of the sea, and Maxim's voice echoing in the cave where he had talked about the woman he loved. Nowhere else but in that pagan place would he have talked of the love that had no beginning, no end, and which might never be fulfilled.

She found a vase in a cupboard and filled it with water. As she arranged Michael's flowers on her dressing-table, she could hear the orchestra tuning up. There was a sound of voices, a patter of feet going towards the wings, and she guessed that the *corps de ballet* were assembling for the curtain-raiser.

Her heart began to beat unevenly. In less than half an hour she would be making for the stage, but right now she must keep occupied. She lacquered her dark hair into place, ready for the crest of leaves and flowers, and made sure the ribbons of her new slippers were sewn on correctly. The slippers were like a supple second skin on her feet, and she was tying the ribbons when the dresser came hurrying in to help her into her costume.

Few alterations had been necessary, and it had been skilfully cleaned and ironed to bring out the colours of the bodice embroidery and to restore the flounce to the skirt of net over silk. The lace on the little apron had turned to the colour of ivory.

At last the costume and headdress were adjusted to the dresser's satisfaction, and she stood back to admire the English ballerina. She clasped her hands against her motherly bosom, and though her Venetian eyes were warm, they were also concerned. Lauri caught the meaning of what she was saying, that the English *signorina* looked charming but so pale. Was she all right? Not sick, or faint?

Lauri was afraid. She was in costume, and in sheer terror of what lay ahead of her. She wasn't only dancing a major role for the first time in her life, but she was replacing an established dancer.

She thought fearfully of what Andreya had said about the scorn of an audience . . . the scorn that was almost as terrible as the panic of one. Her legs went weak, but she couldn't sit down for fear of crushing her costume. Her heart hammered, right in her throat, as footsteps sounded on the floor of the passage outside. Knuckles rapped her door.

'The *Direttore*!' The dresser turned eagerly to the door and opened it.

Maxim came in, tall, dark and distinguished in his evening suit. 'Ah, you are dressed.' There was a curious sternness about him as he came over to her and made her pirouette before him for his inspection. He turned at last to the dresser and complimented her on a job well done. She looked pleased, and after wishing the English *signorina* a big success, she left them alone in the dressing-room with its musky scent of greasepaint, and sweeter scent of flowers. Maxim took note of those on the dressing-table. 'Who are they from?' he asked.

Lauri told him, and touched the myrtle, almost unaware.

'It is the customary thing to do, to send flowers,' Maxim said, in that curiously stern voice. 'I thought I would bring mine.'

She looked at him with bewildered eyes, for the only

flower about him was the small red carnation in his buttonhole. A faint smile came into his eyes as he put a hand into his pocket and withdrew a flat leather case. He sprang the catch and revealed on a bed of satin a brooch in the form of a flower spray. The flowers were glimmering pearl daisies on stems of gold, with leaves of delicate green enamel. It was simple, but so exquisitely wrought that Lauri knew it must be an antique and worth a lot of money.

'You won't be able to wear it to dance in,' said Maxim. 'We don't want Lonza wounding himself on it. Wear it later for the first-night party.'

'It's beautiful, *signor*.' Lauri touched a finger to the tiny carved leaves. 'I shall be pleased to wear it.'

'And to keep it, I hope.'

'To – keep it?' Her great eyes, outlined by stage make-up, met his in confusion. 'Oh, I don't think I could do that.'

'Why not?' He asked the question in a quite pleasant, impersonally interested tone of voice. Not at all the tone of voice of a man offering a girl a priceless brooch.

'Because it's valuable,' she replied. 'If it was pretty but worthless – well, that would be a different matter entirely.'

'It would indeed,' he agreed. 'I would never offer you anything that was worthless, and I don't thank you for offering me such an excuse for not accepting it. You will accept it because I want you to, and because there is no one else it would suit quite so well.'

'What about Venetia?' The words were out before Lauri could stop them. She blushed vividly as his dark eyes narrowed and flashed with a kind of leashed fire over her triangular face with its emphasized features. Her face, her slim bare neck, her shoulders partly revealed by the peasant blouse, caught the fire of his raking glance.

'What about Venetia?' The question winged back at her, barbed and dangerous.

'If the brooch is a – a family one, ought you to give it away – to anyone else?' Lauri drew away from him as she spoke, a slim, bare-shouldered figure whose heart was knocking against the silk of the blouse she wore.

He drew near as she backed away, tall, black-browed, with a mouth in which restraint was at war with strong emotions. He slid the brooch case back into his pocket, and just as quickly took her by the shoulders. His hands were warm against her skin.

'Now is not the time for us to discuss love, or its demands and its dues,' he said quietly. 'In a few short minutes you will be due on stage. How do you feel, child?'

'Frightened,' she said, and at once his hands tightened, as though as he was trying with his touch to imbue her with his own strength and confidence. 'When you go out on that stage you will be taking with you the hopes of your aunt who could not be with you, the good wishes of everyone in the company, and my belief in you as a dancer,' he said firmly. 'When you go out on that stage, you will be Giselle, not Lauri Garner. You will forget your audience, you will forget the theatre, you will remember only that you are a girl to whom nothing matters but the love you feel and want to express.

'Laurina,' now he took her face into his hands and tilted it towards him . . . he used Venetia's name for her almost caressingly, 'you must not be afraid of anything. I shall be only a few feet away from you all the time . . . you trust me, don't you? You know I would never ask you to do anything which I did not feel was in your heart, waiting to be given? Giselle is in you, waiting to be given to all those who love ballet.'

'All those who love ballet,' she echoed. She thought of Aunt Pat, who would be thinking of her through every movement of the ballet . . . who would be so proud if at the end of it she had danced a little magic into the hearts of those who had watched her.

She looked into Maxim's eyes, and a smile came stealing to her lips. 'I am glad you will be watching me from the wings, *signor*,' she said. 'I do trust you.'

'Yes, trust me,' he spoke deeply, almost urgently. 'Whatever I do, I have your best interests at heart.'

He stood back then and took one more considering look at her in the costume which had belonged to his grandmother. 'Come,' he took her by the hand, 'it is time for you to take your place for the opening scene.'

She walked with him towards the sound of the music. Her heart was throbbing. She was hot and chill with the strange unreality of these moments.

Maxim would never know that at the last moment, when the music paused for her to run forward out of Giselle's cottage, she wanted instead to run into his arms and be locked there for ever. Even as this revelation came to her, she was out on the stage of the Fenice and gazing into a reddish-darkness hung with shadowy outlines and jewel-toned exit lights.

There was an intense silence, and then a thrill of music rising from the pit below her poised feet. The music touched the tips of her toes, and then her limbs reacted as though from the left of her someone pulled a string.

A heart-string, for as she briefly turned her head she saw Maxim, tall and dark in the wings. He smiled in his grave, dark-eyed way, and Lauri knew from the

depths of her being that she had to give him all that
he wanted from her . . . the ballerina, not the woman.

The excitement throughout the theatre was electrical
when the curtain came down on the first half of the
ballet. Giselle, mad with love, had killed herself on
Albrecht's sword. When the curtain rose again she
would be one of the Wilis, maidens who live on in the
spirit because they have died unfulfilled by love.

Michael caught Lauri to him in the passage to the
dressing-rooms. 'You darling!' He kissed her exultantly.
'Nijinka, you have never danced as you are dancing
tonight. My sweet witch, are you in love . . . are you
in love with me?'

'Michael, you fool . . .' she broke away from him,
half laughing, half crying with nervous tension and
excitement. 'I must go and change – '

'Lauri, you were marvellous. All those people love
you as much as I do.'

She glanced back and caught the gleam in his eyes.
She fled precipitately to her dressing-room, aware that
her quickened senses had charged their *scènes d'amour*
with a certain reality. Dear heaven! She leaned back
against the door of her dressing-room and caught her
breath. She felt a terrible, strangling ache for Maxim.
It daggered through her body into her bones, a painful
moment of aliveness.

In his Venetian tower she had loved him and not
known. On the island where Venetia was staying she
had learned of the love in which she could have no
share.

She drew away from the door as someone tried the
handle. Her dresser came hurrying in, all smiles. Everyone was talking about the ballet. The *Direttore* was

surrounded by people, and she had not liked to hand to him what he had pulled out of his pocket with the handkerchief to mop his brow.

Lauri stared at the small oblong envelope. 'I'll give it to him,' she said, and held out her hand for it. Automatically she glanced at the name and address on the front of the envelope.

Her name!

The dresser was bustling about laying out the filmy Wili costume and the small coronet of flowers . . . she turned at a heart-wrenching sound from Lauri, and saw that she was reading what had been in the envelope.

'*Signorina*,' the dresser came hurrying over to Lauri in quick concern, 'you are not feeling so good?'

Lauri was stunned, shocked, filled with a silent crying out against what the telegram held. Aunt Pat had been taken into hospital last night . . . and Maxim had withheld the news from her because tonight all her thought and feeling must be given to his precious ballet.

She refolded the telegram, and like a creature in a trance let herself be dressed for the final act of the ballet that meant more to Maxim than anything else. Outside in the passage there was a rustling of satin slippers and chiffon skirts as the *corps de ballet* hurried towards the wings. When she joined them, their white ranks parted to let her through to where Maxim stood. There was something so deeply hurt about her that no one spoke as she handed Maxim a small oblong envelope.

'Where did you get this?' His eyes held a queer dark blaze as he gazed down at Lauri.

'It fell out of your pocket and my dresser picked it up.' Her voice was as cold as her eyes. 'My name was on the envelope, so I read what was inside.'

'My dear – '

'No,' she threw out a hand, indicating the stage, the sets, the groups of dancers, 'all this is what is dear to you. You live for it, and the illness of other people must not be allowed to interfere with it. I think I hate you Maxim. Tonight I should have been on my way home to Aunt Pat, *not dancing*!'

'I knew you would feel that way.' He drew her firmly into the green room at the side of the stage and closed the door. He stood with his back to it, and he seemed to Lauri to have a look of utter determination as she swept her eyes over him.

'Don't try to understand my motives,' he said, 'just believe that I was doing what I thought was best for you.'

'For the ballet,' she cried back. 'For the launching of your second Travilla – and you've succeeded, haven't you, Maxim? Everyone out there is saying all the things you wanted them to say – '

'You have succeeded as well,' he cut in. 'Don't you realize that?'

'I never wanted fame, bright lights, the roar of the crowd,' she said, scorn dying away and leaving her tired.

'I was not referring to any of that,' he said quietly. 'Each time you danced, Lauri, a pair of ghosts danced at your heels. Their fingers reached out of flames and caught at your feet – but tonight you broke free of your ghosts and forgot your fears. Don't you realize that in doing that you have proved to a brave and selfless woman that she did the right thing in letting you leave her to come here . . . and dance?'

'You persuaded her that it was the right thing for her to do,' Lauri threw back at him. 'I think you knew all the time that she was ill – far more ill than she let on to me.'

'Yes, I knew,' he admitted. 'She told me of her own fears, and her doctor's, but she wanted you to have the chance to become a great dancer. She believed it was in you to dance as you have danced tonight. Are you now going to let her down and prove that you grew up for one hour only?'

'No, *signor.*' Lauri looked at him and saw again a stranger to whom she could never get close. 'And now I think you had better let me go. I am sure you wouldn't like it if I missed my cue.'

He stood aside from the door and opened it for her. As she walked past him her ballerina dress was filmy and pale about her slim, withdrawn figure. 'I shall fly home tomorrow to my aunt,' she said. 'She needs me.'

'Very well.' He inclined his head, and his eyes were inscrutable as she ran in her satin slippers to take her place among the Wilis – the maidens unfulfilled by love.

There was not a murmur, not a movement in all that packed theatre. Each pair of eyes was fixed upon the thin young dancer with the great honey-coloured eyes and wounded mouth. She was so without defence, blown about the stage by the cross-currents of love, betrayal, the whims and cruelties of other people – people she had trusted.

She soared alone, and then in the arms of her partner . . . heart, limbs and spirit took wing and the elusive essence of romance was alive again for every woman in the audience; every man who yearned to believe again in innocence.

Moments during that *pas de deux* were sensitive almost beyond endurance, and somewhere in the auditorium a woman gave a compulsive sob. To love as that girl was loving Albrecht! His lean, dark face in her hands, her eyes tortured because their love must be for ever unfulfilled.

Lauri's anguish at heart was in her dancing. And Michael, a witness to that scene in the wings between her and Maxim, was tender and strong with her . . . the little Nijinka who was not for him.

Came inevitably the moment of farewell between Giselle and Albrecht, and as he collapsed to his knees, and buried his face in the lilies on her tomb, a murmur as of a coming storm began to arise from the auditorium. It pulsed in the air. There was a moment like that of a stopped heart, and then a convulsive catching of breath as the applause broke out like thunder.

'*Bravo . . . Bravissimo!*'

It roared, and the two slim figures were bowed down by its force . . . there was a wetness on Lauri's cheeks . . . tears were raining down her face.

Flowers beat at them. The crowd was cheering. Someone tall, dark, and gravely smiling was standing in the wings, applauding.

Lonza turned and looked at his partner, then he took both her hands and carried them close to his lips. 'Nijinka,' he murmured. He was choked, he could say no more, and the storm seemed to grow louder as he kissed her hands.

'*Bravo . . . Bravissimo!*'

Maxim's triumph was achieved. The air was filled with it, the scent of crushed flowers, and those spilling from Lauri's arms. The cluster of dancers were breathless with excitement, and when at last the curtains closed they surrounded Lauri and after much kissing and embracing Lauri was like a crushed flower herself.

'To your dressing-rooms!' Bruno was among them, scattering them like so many white doves. 'Be off with you! I am sure our little Lauri would like to be alone to rest after her wonderful performance.'

'Thank you, Bruno – ' then beyond his shoulder she saw Maxim approaching, and clutching her flowers she fled to her dressing-room. It was quiet there, but she had no intention of remaining. With fingers that shook she untied the ribbons of her battered slippers and withdrew her feet from them. She gave each aching foot a rub, then slipped into outdoor shoes. She snatched up a towel and wiped the make-up from her face . . . she was buttoning her coat over her ballet dress as she made her way swiftly and silently out of a side door of the theatre.

A fairly thick mist was wafting up out of the water and half shrouding the city. Walking through it added to Lauri's sense of being adrift between triumph and despair.

She merged into the shadows, her hands plunged into her pockets, her eyes tearless now in tired hollows. 'I think I hate you . . . hate you.' The words echoed in her mind. 'Ballet is what is dear to you, you live for it.'

She came to a bridge and walked wearily across to the middle of it. There was a hollow lap of water against stone, and slow curls of mist rose about her and touched her cheeks like cold fingers. She shivered, and though she knew it was foolhardy to stand here in the misty cold after dancing in a warm theatre, she couldn't make the effort to go back.

Overhead the moon lost and found itself among the clouds. A gondola cut through the misty water and swept past the old palaces, and warehouses. Past the stone angels that never slept, and the satyrs that kept watch through the night. The water murmured in the wake of the black boat, and from a waterfront café drifted the sound of a Venetian song.

Come tomorrow, come quickly. The music seemed to set itself to the refrain in Lauri's mind. Let me hurry home to tell Aunt Pat that all I ever wanted was love. That to be a great dancer was the dream of others, not my dream.

She turned then to leave the bridge, and saw someone striding out of the mist towards her. She moved back slowly until the parapet of the bridge brought her up short. Her face was a strained triangle, her mist-wet hair clung to her thin young neck. 'Go away,' she said. 'I've had enough for one evening.'

'Do you really imagine I would go away and leave you here?' he asked. His face looked grim. 'What a childish thing to do, to run out of the theatre in a flimsy dress and coat – it was a good thing the doorman saw you and could tell me which direction you had taken. Knowing how you like bridges, it seemed reasonable to suppose that you would come and mope on this one.'

'Mope?' she echoed. 'Is that what you call it, when my aunt lies ill in hospital and you keep the news from me – just for the sake of your blasted ballet?'

'What good would it have done your aunt if you had moped all over the *palazzo* tonight instead of dancing *Giselle*? Knowing about your triumph will help her to get well, I am sure of that. I was sending a wire to the hospital when you ran out of the theatre in such a foolish hurry.'

'Oh,' she said, and gazed at him with wide eyes as he put a hand to her damp hair and felt it.

'You really are a child,' he said, and closed a protective arm about her. 'I see the lights of a café on the

other side of this bridge. Let us go there and have some
hot coffee.'

'That would be nice.' They began to walk across the
bridge towards the soft lights of the café, and the music.
His arm felt warm and strong about her, and so secure.
'Thank you for sending a wire to Aunt Pat, *signor*. It
was kind of you.'

'I can be kind.' She felt him glance down at her, and
caught the sardonic note in his voice. 'It quite shocked
Venetia that you should think me heartless.'

'Not heartless – exactly.' Lauri forced a laugh to cover
the tears in her voice. 'But Venetia has seen more of
your – your loving side than I have.'

'I don't quite follow your reasoning.' He stopped
walking and turned her to face him on the misty bridge.
'Why should Venetia know more about that side of me
than anyone else?'

'Because you love her,' Lauri said simply.

She heard him catch his breath, and then caught hers
as his hands tightened painfully on her arms. 'I have
known Venetia for a long time, she is a very good friend
of mine, but where could you have got the idea that
I love her?'

'You said you did, the day we went to the Villa
Nora.' Lauri was shaking with nerves, coldness, his nearness and her fear of giving herself away to him. She
tried to pull away from him, but the more she pulled
the firmer grew his grip until she found herself right
up against him.

'That day on the island – you said the woman you
loved was on the island.' Her heart was pounding, for
his hands were slipping up her sides and one arm was
curving round to hold her. '*Signor* – please –'

'Please, do what?' he mocked. 'Were you jealous when

I said the woman I loved was on that island? I hope you were, *carina*, for often I have felt jealous.'

'You?' she gasped, her hair in a stream over his arm as he bent to her, smiling in the brilliant way that must have ravished her heart long ago.

'I can be jealous and fierce and all the things that a man is with the woman he loves.' His eyes held hers and searched them as the mist drifted about them and everything was muffled but the pounding of her heart . . . and his.

Maxim's heart, joined to hers and beating into her, heaven riven in two as his mouth in sudden impatient hunger crushed to nothing all her questions, and supplied all the answers.

'You were on that island, were you not?' he whispered fiercely. 'I wanted then to kiss you awake, into a woman, but first you had to dance and lose those fears from your childhood. That was why I was ruthless with you, why I made you dance tonight. I will never make you dance again, my love, if you don't want to.'

She smiled and rested against his shoulder, and felt his lips brush her temple. 'I must dance in London for Aunt Pat,' she said softly. 'You won't mind, Maxim, if I go to her tomorrow?'

'I am coming with you,' he said at once.

'But what about the company?' Lauri looked at him in such sheer amazement that he burst out laughing.

'Bruno can take care of the company. For now, my love, you are my first consideration. For always, come to that.'

'For always?' The words sounded so lovely, so secure, so rich with promise. 'Oh, Maxim!'

'You want to belong to me for always?'

She nodded, and suddenly shy of his dark, handsome,

worldly eyes, she pressed her face to his chest. 'How is it possible that you love me?' she whispered. 'I'm so naive about a lot of things, and you're so wise. You know so much. Won't I bore you?'

'Naive is the word,' he mocked gently. 'As I warned you once before, don't ever change, *carina*. I love you exactly as you are, all heart, nonsense and innocence. So innocent, my pet. Too unspoiled to know that I meant to have you from the first moment I looked at you.'

His left eyebrow quirked above a wicked dark eye. 'You would not have been able to run fast enough if you had known that, eh?'

'What if I had fallen in love with someone else?' she teased in her turn.

'The gods would not have been that unkind to me, after I waited so long to find someone like you. You are everything to me, Laurina. Your every gesture, every smile and dancing step is dear to me.'

And there on that old Venetian bridge, where lovers had kissed down the centuries, Lauri and her love pledged their love in the old, old way.

A gondola sped beneath the bridge, and the voice of the gondolier rose rich on the misty air. Marry young, girl. Marry while the leaf is green. . . .

Mills & Boon
Best Seller Romances

The very best of Mills & Boon
brought back for those of you
who missed reading them when they
were first published.
There are three other Best Seller Romances
for you to collect this month.

ETERNAL SUMMER
by Anne Hampson

Greece, the land of the ancient gods and of eternal summer;
all its beauty spots — Delphi, Athens, the glittering islands; all
these were to be part of Marika's daily life — if she agreed to
Nickolas Loukas's strange proposal. But would the price be
too high?

THE TOWER OF THE WINDS
by Elizabeth Hunter

When her sister died, Charity was determined to take care of
her baby son — but the child's uncle, the masterful Greek
Loukos Papandreous, was equally determined that the baby
was going to remain in Greece — with him. How could Charity
cope with this man who insisted that, as she was a woman,
her opinions were of no account — yet who made her more
and more glad she was a woman?

MAN IN A MILLION
by Roberta Leigh

Harriet wrote a best-seller and was given the chance of pro-
ducing it as a million-dollar movie. But Joel Blake, the owner
of the studio, believed that women were unfitted for such
work and made his opinion plain. Did it really matter to
Harriet what he thought? As time went by it appeared that
it did?

If you have difficulty in obtaining any of these books through
your local paperback retailer, write to:

Mills & Boon Reader Service
P.O. Box 236, Thornton Road, Croydon, Surrey, CR9 3RU.

Mills & Boon
Best Seller Romances

The very best of Mills & Boon Romances
brought back for those of you who missed
them when they were first published.
In October
we bring back the following four
great romantic titles.

THE AUTOCRAT OF MELHURST
by Anne Hampson

Claire had promised Simon Condliffe that she would stay on
in her job as nanny to his small niece as long as he needed her
— but she hadn't bargained on falling in love with him, and
then having to watch him with his close friend — or was she
his fiancée? — Ursula Corwell.

LORD OF ZARACUS
by Anne Mather

When Carolyn joined her archaeologist father in Mexico, she
found herself immediately in conflict with Don Carlos, who
owned the valley where her father was searching for a Zapotec
city. Don Carlos thought she was 'a typical product of the
permissive society' and Carolyn let him know that 'I am not
one of your peons'. It seemed an inauspicious beginning to
their relationship. And yet—

LOGAN'S ISLAND
by Mary Wibberley

Helen had inherited an island off the coast of Brazil — jointly
with an unknown man called Jake Logan. Its name — Island
of Storms — just about summed up the wildly antagonistic
relationship that promptly developed between the two of
them!

LOVE'S PRISONER
by Violet Winspear

Meeting Lafe Sheridan proved a milestone in Eden's young
life, and she knew that no man would ever mean as much to
her. But her beautiful sister had more effect on him . . . He
was rich and lonely, and Gale had always meant to marry a
rich man . . .

If you have difficulty in obtaining any of these books through
your local paperback retailer, write to:

Mills & Boon Reader Service
P.O. Box 236, Thornton Road, Croydon, Surrey, CR9 3RU.